The Cowboy's Promise

TERESA SOUTHWICK

HARLEQUIN

SPECIAL
EDITION

Special thanks and acknowledgment are given to Teresa Southwick for her contribution to the Montana Mavericks: What Happened to Beatrix? miniseries.

Recycling programs for this product may not exist in your area.

ISBN-13: 978-1-335-89483-0

The Cowboy's Promise

Copyright © 2020 by Harlequin Books S.A.

This edition published by arrangement with Harlequin Books S.A.

For questions and comments about the quality of this book, please contact us at CustomerService@Harlequin.com.

Harlequin Enterprises ULC
22 Adelaide St. West, 40th Floor
Toronto, Ontario M5H 4E3, Canada
www.Harlequin.com

Printed in U.S.A.

Teresa Southwick lives with her husband in Las Vegas, the city that reinvents itself every day. An avid fan of romance novels, she is delighted to be living out her dream of writing for Harlequin.

Books by Teresa Southwick

Harlequin Special Edition

An Unexpected Partnership
What Makes a Father
Daughter on His Doorstep

The Bachelors of Blackwater Lake

A Decent Proposal
The Widow's Bachelor Bargain
How to Land Her Lawman
A Word with the Bachelor
Just a Little Bit Married
The New Guy in Town
His by Christmas
Just What the Cowboy Needed

Montana Mavericks: Six Brides for Six Brothers

Maverick Holiday Magic

Montana Mavericks: The Lonelyhearts Ranch

Unmasking the Maverick

Montana Mavericks: The Baby Bonanza

Her Maverick M.D.

Visit the Author Profile page
at Harlequin.com for more titles.

To readers who adore happy endings as much as I do. Without you I couldn't do the job I love. Though it doesn't seem like enough, this thank-you comes from the bottom of my heart.

Chapter One

There's no place like home. And for Erica Abernathy home was Bronco Heights, Montana—where everyone had an opinion, and not always a positive one.

She was driving her loaded-to-the-roof SUV down the road to the big house on the Ambling A Ranch, where she'd grown up. The trip from Denver had been long, but now that she was so close, she wouldn't mind a couple thousand more miles between her and what was coming.

She loved her family, but wasn't looking forward to their reaction when they saw her. There would be so many questions.

Although that happened every time she came

home for a visit. Usually some variation of "Do you like *city* life in Denver?" Or "Are you dating anyone? Getting serious about a special man?" And the ever popular, "Can we look forward to an engagement soon? We can't wait to be grandparents." Erica glanced down at her pregnant belly that was getting closer to the steering wheel every day.

"You're going to make them grandparents, little one. But they are not going to be happy with me."

Erica stopped her car in front of the large home constructed from Canadian red cedar and native Montana rock. The building materials were a salute to pioneers and the generations of Abernathys who came before and settled this land. Sturdy logs supported the second story roof over the front entrance. The sun had just set, and inside lights blazed through the tall windows.

There was a chimney sticking up over the pitched roofline and smoke drifted out of it. She could picture the fireplace in the great room, where flames would crackle and snap. That wasn't about providing atmosphere. Montana could get darn cold, and it wasn't unheard of to have a freak snowstorm the beginning of October. Shivering, she pulled her poncho up more snugly around her neck.

She'd missed this place. In spite of what her family thought about her choosing a career in Colorado over it, she did love the ranch, the land, the mountains. And after twelve years, she was back to stay, just like her parents always wanted. But when Angela and George Abernathy saw her, they were probably not going to ask about city life in Denver. They would have way too many other questions.

She sighed. Procrastination wasn't going to make this first step any easier. "Here goes nothing..."

She walked up to the front door and rang the bell. It was her childhood home, but she hadn't told them she was coming. It didn't feel right to simply walk in.

Suddenly the front porch light flashed on, the door was opened and Angela Abernathy stood there. She was in her early fifties with dark blond highlighted hair. Her blue eyes widened and she blinked once, then smiled with pleasure. "Erica! Sweetheart, what a surprise."

"Hi, Mama."

"This is wonderful. Don't stand out here in the cold. Come inside. Please tell me you're staying. And for more than a day this time."

"Big fat yes." She forced cheerfulness into her voice. "I definitely am."

"Is there a holiday I don't know about?"

Boom, there it was. First judgment. The subtext was that since her grandparents' funerals five years ago she only showed up on holidays and hadn't visited since last Christmas. And her mom hadn't yet noticed the main attraction.

"Why didn't you tell us you were coming?" She

pulled her daughter close for a hug, then backed away, looking shocked. "Erica?"

She walked farther into the brightly lit entryway and pulled her poncho off over her head. Her mother's eyes went wide and her jaw actually dropped. In her rebellious teens, there was a time when Erica might have taken pride in pulling off the miracle of rendering her unflappable mother speechless. Not so much now. Or like this.

"You're pregnant." Her mother stated the obvious. "*Very* pregnant. Why didn't you tell us you're going to have a baby?"

Her token teen mutinies were small potatoes compared to this, but every time Erica had disappointed her parents, it ripped her heart out. This was, pardon the pun, the mother of all rebellions and no matter how old she was, or how much career success she had, making them proud was always her intention.

"I was going to tell you—" No points for good intentions. She lifted her hands in a helpless gesture. "I couldn't figure out how to say it."

Angela's gaze dropped to the ring finger on her left hand. "Is there a marriage you couldn't figure out how to tell us about either?"

Erica flinched at the words. Not that her mother's tone was sharp, but because it wasn't. The hurt in her eyes and reproach in her voice were like pokes in the chest, jabbing her heart. This was why she'd put off the conversation. The problem was, the longer she had dragged her feet, the worse it got. That was her bad, just one on a very long list.

"No, Mama. I'm not married."

"Is it Peter's baby?"

Erica should have expected the question but hadn't. "No. I told you we broke up over a year ago."

Regret was stark in her mom's eyes. "You did but I just thought—" The breakup had stunned Erica because they'd dated for a long time. Peter Barron was handsome, smart, fun, successful and she'd really cared about him. They had a relationship that was the envy of all their friends. She'd been so sure he was The One. So, she brought up the subject of having children. His answer was adamant and unequivocal: he didn't want any kids. Ever. And he wasn't going to change his mind.

She'd tried to tell herself it didn't matter. She could be content, fulfilled and live a happy life with Peter while having a successful career of her own. It could be enough. But every time she saw a pregnant woman or a baby in a stroller, she got a knot of emptiness and longing in her stomach. Like a protest from her uterus. The yearning for a baby, the ache to be a mother, just wouldn't go away.

"Erica, who is the father?"

The quiet question snapped her back to the present. "I don't want to talk about it."

The anxiety in her mother's blue eyes increased,

and her face went pale. "Did something happen to you?"

"No." She reached out, took her mother's hand and Angela squeezed it hard. "I didn't mean to scare you."

She'd given her poor mother a lot of shocks since she walked through the front door. Maybe she should tell her the truth. It was possible that she would understand. Angela Abernathy had two babies in two years, a boy and a girl. She thought her family was complete. Then right around the time she turned thirty, she accidentally got pregnant and realized how very much she wanted another baby. But she miscarried and the loss was devastating. After several more tries and losses she was told she couldn't carry a baby. It nearly destroyed her.

When Erica was suddenly staring thirty in the face, she remembered her mother's difficulty with pregnancy. Erica had no potential husband material on her horizon and worried that the inability to carry a baby at a certain age was genetic. She wasn't willing to wait and hope for a man to come along. She wouldn't risk what might be her only chance and pulled the trigger on going the single mom route. A big part of her hadn't believed IUI—intrauterine insemination—would work, but it did, and she was thrilled.

If anyone would understand the primal longing to have a baby, it was this woman.

"Mama, I really want to talk to you about this—"

The sound of heavy footsteps coming closer stopped her. Before she saw him, Erica heard her father's voice.

"Angela? What's taking so long? Who was at the door?" And then George Abernathy walked into the entryway and saw her. Emotions swirled in his eyes from pleasure to shock.

"Surprise." She'd always been Daddy's little girl, but she'd never seen him look at her quite like this before.

He was fit and tan but the color drained from his face. "Good Lord, Erica. What in the world—"

"You're going to be a grandfather, Daddy." She tried to smile, but her mouth was trembling and her heart was beating way too fast.

"Did you come here alone?"

"You're asking if I'm married. The answer is no."

He waited for several moments, then rubbed a hand across the back of his neck. "Are you all right? You look well."

Erica was pretty sure telling him the details would make things worse. Her father was old-fashioned and set in his ways. She knew her brother, Gabe, had butted heads with him over trying progressive ranching techniques. *Stubborn* was her dad's middle name, and Gabe finally gave up. Now he was more involved with real estate wheeling and dealing than the ranch. No, admitting to her father that she'd gone to a sperm bank was the last thing she planned to do.

"I'm fine, Daddy."

He looked down for a moment as if gathering his thoughts. Then he met her gaze and his eyes churned with confusion and hurt. "We're your parents and we have concerns—"

"I know. And I love you both very much," she interrupted. "But please believe me when I say I'm fine. Obviously I'm going to be a mother and more happy about this pregnancy than I can even put into words. I will do my very best to do as spectacular a job with my child as you guys did with Gabe and me. When the shock wears off, I hope you'll be as excited about this baby as I am. I know how much you want to be grandparents."

Neither of them responded to her impassioned speech but simply stared at her. Then they looked at each other and seemed to exchange silent agreement not to say anything more.

Finally her mother asked, "How long are you staying?"

"Would it be all right if I lived here until I find a job?"

"Of course you can stay with us—" Then her father stopped as her words sank in. "Wait. You left Barron Enterprises?" George Abernathy didn't shock easily, but this was the second time in five minutes he'd looked completely bewildered.

Erica was on a roll apparently. "I was fired actually."

"I don't understand. Not long ago you got that big promotion," her mom protested.

"I did." To chief administrative officer. In the last few years, these two had been so busy quizzing her about her marriage prospects, she hadn't been sure the move up the corporate ladder had even registered with them. "But Mr. Barron Senior, called me into his office to tell me I was being transferred to the Miami office. I didn't want to go."

"Why would he do that?" her dad asked. "Doesn't the chief administrative officer work out of the corporate office in Denver?"

Wow, she thought. He really had been paying attention. She'd been hoping to gloss over this part. "Peter married one of the receptionists at work. And she's pregnant." Even though she didn't love him anymore, that news had come as a blow. The lying bastard. "His wife has been a little hostile to me, since everyone at the company knows he and I were together for a long time."

"You said he's not the baby's father," Angela reminded her.

"He's not. But the woman apparently had a problem seeing me every day."

"So, Peter's father fired you because the new wife is an insecure twit?" her mother scoffed.

Erica was glad they seemed to be annoyed with someone besides her. "Apparently."

"That's wrongful termination," her father chimed in. "You can't let them get away with that."

"Way ahead of you, Daddy. I already have an appointment with an attorney."

"Good for you," he said.

"The thing is, after I moved in with Peter I sold my condo and banked a nice profit. When we split up, I rented an apartment while I figured out what I wanted to do." And how big a place she would need *if* she got pregnant. "I have savings, but no job means no income until I can find another one. There's no telling how long that will be, so my savings have to last."

Her father nodded his understanding. "And if you file a lawsuit against Barron Enterprises, it could be a long time until there's a financial settlement."

"Exactly. So, I was hoping you guys wouldn't mind if I stayed here until I get back on my feet," she said.

"Of course." He didn't hesitate. "You're back where you belong. Even if it means coming home with your tail between your legs."

Erica refused to flinch at the words. Her father was right. She'd thought she had everything figured out and was thrown a big curve. She refused to call it a mess because that reflected on the child she was carrying, and the choices had been hers. The way it had played out made her feel like crap, and now she needed help from the family she'd neglected.

"Thank you, Daddy."

Her dad nodded, held out his arms to her and she stepped into them for a much needed hug. "I love you, honey. I think I speak for your mother when I say we're glad you're home, but we aren't finished talking about this baby's father."

Erica was finished, but wisely chose not to say that. The line was drawn in the sand, and she knew which side of it she was on.

Her dad helped her unload the car and take some things upstairs to her old room. She appreciated that very much and knew all of this must be hard for him. After that, she felt an overwhelming need to see her big brother. Fortunately his house was on the ranch and was located not far from her parents, so Erica walked over.

For the second time that day, she knocked on a door and waited to shock the person who opened it. But she was the one who got a surprise when a pretty, petite woman with long, straight blond hair stood there instead of her big brother.

"Hi. I'm Melanie Driscoll."

"You're the woman who's going to marry my brother. I'm Erica." She couldn't believe they hadn't met. "Mom called me right after he proposed, and she said the ring is fabulous."

"I think so." Melanie held out her left hand with a platinum band supporting a spectacularly large diamond.

"Gorgeous." Erica smiled. "When's the wedding?"

"Next summer."

"I'm so glad to finally meet you."

"Same here." The other woman's gaze dropped to her belly. "And I hear congratulations are in order for you, too. Your mom called."

"I figured."

Melanie shrugged. "Gabe is still on the phone with her."

"My ears were burning," Erica said wryly, and slid off her poncho as she stepped into the warm house.

Melanie gave her the once-over. "I've known you all of a minute but I have to say, you're positively glowing. The baby bump is so cute and you're beautiful."

"You should probably get your eyes checked. I'm as big as a barn."

"Hardly. When is the baby due?"

"November."

"You look fantastic," Melanie said. "How do you feel?"

"The first three months were a little rough with morning sickness. But since then I've been great. Not too tired. I love being pregnant." She smiled at the other woman. "I've known you all of a minute, but I have to say this. I'm so glad my brother has the good sense to marry you."

"I'm the lucky one. I'd given up on finding someone and then, there he was." She turned an adoring gaze on the man in question when he came up beside her.

Gabriel Abernathy was a tall, broad-shouldered force of nature. When he looked at Melanie, his blue eyes were flirty. Then his gaze landed on Erica and turned serious.

"I just got off the phone with Mom."

"Hello to you, too," she said.

"Come here." He held out his arms.

She walked into them and sighed when he hugged her. "I'm so glad to see you."

"Same here. But I have to ask—what the hell are you doing, Erica?"

"I'm having a baby." She put her hands protectively on her belly. "And I want this child more than anything in the world."

"Mom told me you won't say who the father is." With his hands on his hips and looking all serious at her, Gabe looked a lot like their father.

It had been a long, emotional day, and Erica was just about at her limit. "Don't you start on me. I left for Colorado to go to college. I stayed to have a career. Every time I make a decision, I'm being judged in a bad way. And you all wonder why I don't come home more often."

"It's not judgment. It's just that—" he dragged his hand through his spiky dirty blond hair "we miss you. Me. Mom. Dad. Grandpa Alexander. Gramps."

Guilt zinged her hard. Gramps—her great-grandfather, Josiah Abernathy—was in his mid-nineties and had been diagnosed with dementia. The subtext of her brother's words was that no one knew how much time he had left and she'd been focused on career which didn't leave a lot of free time.

She pushed the guilt away. "I was entitled to a life that *I* chose. Not Mom and Dad. They wouldn't have been happy with anything but me marrying a local rancher. I wanted more. To travel. Broaden my horizons."

"And you did." Again he glanced at her belly. "But you've lost time with Gramps. Precious time. And he doesn't say much at all anymore."

"I'll go see him soon—" A lump in her throat cut off more words. She did love Gramps and felt badly that he was declining. There was no good excuse except that life happened. One day turned into the next and before she'd realized it, twelve years had gone by.

Erica didn't want to fight with her brother. She'd come here to get away from the tension at the big house. That thought pulled her up short. Wasn't that what they called prison? It was time to change the subject.

"So, tell me how you and Melanie met," she said enthusiastically.

"Mel moved to Bronco from Rust Creek Falls for a job. She ended up looking into the Abernathy family history. Gramps's history."

So much for a subject change, Erica thought. But Gabe was smiling lovingly at his fiancée. And this was the happiest she'd ever seen him look.

"How did that happen, Melanie?"

"It's Mel," she corrected, then her expression turned from tender to concerned. "I have a good friend in Rust Creek Falls named Winona Cobbs. It came to my attention that she and Josiah Abernathy were secretly in love when they were very young. She got pregnant. When she gave birth, she thought the little girl was stillborn and had a breakdown. But that's not what happened. The baby was alive."

Gabe jumped into the story. "It turned out that Gramps's parents forced him to leave town and put the baby up for adoption. We think somewhere in or around Bronco."

"Oh my God." Erica couldn't believe what she was hearing. "How did you find all this out?"

"When the Ambling A Ranch in Rust Creek Falls was sold, the new people found Josiah's journal in the house. There was a letter inside to Winona. Somehow he found out who adopted their daughter, Beatrix, and promised he'd find a way to bring her back to Winona."

Erica was holding her breath. Waiting for the happy reunion part of the story. When it didn't come, she said, "And?"

"Because of the dementia, he can't give us any information. A friend of mine who's really good with social media did an internet search with what information we have and got a hit." Melanie looked up at Gabe, and disappointment was all over their faces. "It turned out that was just someone looking for money."

"People like that make me so angry." Not only that, Erica was feeling even more guilty about neglecting her great-grandfather. "What now?"

"Good question," Mel said. "So far we've only turned up frauds and weirdos."

Erica looked at her and saw concern. "There's more, isn't there?"

"Winona was hospitalized recently. She's ninety-three and frail. I'm worried that if something doesn't break soon, we'll lose her before we can reunite her with her daughter."

"That would be awful. What are we going to do?" Erica demanded.

"What's this 'we' stuff?" he asked.

"I want to help."

"Really?" Gabe looked surprised.

"Yes, me. I'll do whatever I can."

"Why?"

"He's my great-grandfather." And that wasn't her only reason.

Erica was definitely shocked that Josiah had a daughter out of wedlock that the family never knew about. But she felt a parallel to his story. Her own secret. She was having a baby, and no one was going to know how this child came to be.

"I love him," she said simply.

"I know that." But his tone and expression were skeptical, as if he didn't expect her to stick around.

And why would he? She didn't come home enough when her life was going great. Until it fell apart, she'd acted as if she didn't need any of them.

"I know I should have made more of an effort to visit. But I'm here now and I want to do whatever I can to help. I've certainly got time—"

Gabe's expression turned sympathetic. "Mom told me about Peter and his father."

Erica saw the blaze of fury in his eyes but knew that it wasn't directed at her. She loved him so much for that.

She let out a sigh. "It's been an emotional and eventful couple of weeks."

Mel put her arm around Erica. "You've been through a lot recently. Everyone needs a minute to get used to the new normal. It's all going to be fine."

"Listen to her, baby sister. She's a smart lady." He smiled tenderly at the woman he was going to marry. "And I'm taking her out to dinner tonight."

"Why don't you come with us?" Mel asked her.

"I don't want to intrude."

"You won't be. Right, Gabe?" She turned her big blue eyes on him.

He nodded. "Definitely, you should come. There's a new restaurant in town. Barbecue but better. DJ's Deluxe."

"I'm the CFO now and have connections," Mel said. "Come with us. A change of scene will be good for you. We could all use a distraction."

"I could sure use one."

"It's settled then," Mel declared.

Erica watched her brother hold his fiancée's jacket for her to slip on. He put his arm around her for a quick hug, then took her hand and laced their fingers together.

Oh man, he's got it bad, Erica thought. *The bigger they are, the harder they fall.*

She didn't for a moment regret that she was pregnant, but seeing Mel and Gabe together, loving each other, made her a little envious. On the upside, her baby was going to have the best aunt and uncle in the world.

Chapter Two

Morgan Dalton walked into DJ's Deluxe and went straight to the bar. He needed a beer, and if a woman came along after that, he wouldn't complain. A woman would sure take his mind off his problems.

The place was crowded tonight, but he found a spot at the bar. DJ Traub himself was tending it and delivering food. The man was in his forties, handsome, a friendly guy with a face you could trust. The restaurant owner, who looked like he could just as easily round up a herd of cattle, had dark hair, brown eyes. He put a plate of potato skins deluxe in front of the blond woman sitting beside Morgan.

"This looks fantastic," she said. "Even better than

the supermessy wings I just ate. Everything you give me is better than the last."

"You keep eating, I'll keep the food coming. It's the least I can do for Bronco Heights' newest full-time resident and my CFO's future sister-in-law."

Morgan was eavesdropping, but it wasn't his fault. She was close enough that he could smell her super-sexy perfume. And he liked her voice. There was something low and husky and sensuous about it that made him sit up and take notice of everything she said.

DJ noticed him and said hello. Morgan had been a regular since the place opened, and they'd struck up a friendship.

He angled his head toward the woman beside him, a signal that he'd like to be introduced. The other man nodded slightly, an indication that his message was received.

"Hey, Erica," DJ said. "Since you're new to town, I thought you'd like to meet my friend Morgan Dalton."

Still chewing a bite of potato, she full on looked at him for the first time. That face... *This is what it must feel like to get zapped with those paddle things when your heart stops.*

She was beautiful. He'd seen his share of beautiful women in his thirty-four years, some of them on a movie screen. But this one sitting so close to him was more than a wow. He liked women, they liked him and he did his share of dating, although it was never serious and never would be. But he was dead certain that he'd never had such a strong reaction to a female the very first time he laid eyes on her.

"Hello, Morgan," she said. "I'm Erica."

"Nice to meet you." He barely noticed when DJ put a glass of beer in front of him. He wanted to say *where have you been all my life* and was afraid the words had come out of his mouth. But she didn't look afraid, so he figured he hadn't made a fool of himself yet. "So, you're new to town?"

"Not exactly. But I haven't lived here for twelve years. What about you?"

"I've been here a year." Why did it feel so much longer? "My father bought Dalton's Grange. My four brothers and I work there with my dad."

"There are four more at home like you?" she teased.

Her smile was as spectacular as a Montana sunrise, and he swore his heart got zapped again. "Yes, ma'am."

"How do you like it here, so far?" She cut into the potato skin and ate a piece.

"Prettiest country I've ever seen. But a little on the chilly side." He took a sip from his beer glass. "Could just be me, but there are some folks who consider us new money, without deep roots or any legacy. A couple of families have been here for generations. The Taylors and Abernathys. If you're not one of them, you get some funny looks."

"Really? Thanks for the warning." She nodded her head, but there was a twinkle in her pretty hazel eyes.

"So where are you moving from?" he asked.

"Colorado. Denver. My parents have been wanting me to come back and I had a change of circumstances in my career."

"Oh?"

"I got fired."

Morgan wasn't sure how he knew, but some instinct told him it was not a just termination. "Whoever fired you was clearly an idiot."

"I think so. But that's very nice of you to say, considering that we just met."

"The length of our acquaintance doesn't make my comment any less sincere. I just know. Because… Where have you been all my life?" He couldn't believe the words actually came out of his mouth. "Wait. Forget I said that—"

"No way. I love it." Erica was laughing. "That was quite possibly cheesier than these potato skins."

"I take it back—"

"And without a doubt the sweetest thing a man's ever said to me," she added.

"So that didn't make you want to head for the exit?"

"I'm made of sterner stuff." She smiled her punch-to-the-gut smile again. "Besides, I happen to like cheese."

He met her gaze over the corner of the shiny teak bar that separated them as they sat at a right angle to each other. "That makes two of us."

"So tell me, Morgan, why don't you have a beautiful woman on your arm tonight?"

"I wouldn't say *you're* on my arm exactly," he answered, "but you're talking to me. And you're definitely beautiful."

Her smile was suddenly shy and a little sad for some reason. "But we're not together. A good-looking cowboy like you, in this place all by yourself, is a dozen kinds of wrong. So what gives?"

"I thought I made that clear. I've been waiting for you." He knew he was only half kidding.

"Are you flirting with me?" There was the cutest expression on her face, a look that said the flirt factor might be going both ways.

"Maybe a little," he admitted. "And that makes me want to ask for your phone number. It's not every day a man meets a woman like you."

"That statement is true in more ways than you realize," she said wryly. "And it's becoming clear to me you didn't notice that I'm—"

"What?"

She swiveled her bar stool sideways toward him. The good news was they sat close enough that her legs were touching his. The jaw-dropping news was that she was very much with child.

Morgan glanced from her round belly to her eyes a couple of times before blurting out, "You're pregnant."

"Really?" Her look was wry as she put her hands on her stomach. "I hadn't noticed. But that would explain why I've been eating my weight in food that DJ keeps bringing me, even after I ate dinner."

"I didn't mean it like that. It's just— I didn't mean to offend you." He automatically looked for a ring on her left hand.

"I'm not married or offended." There was laughter in her voice.

"Erica, you have to know that I've never hit on a pregnant woman in my life. I apologize."

"Well, Morgan Dalton, I'm thrilled to be your first. And speaking for pregnant women everywhere, it's quite flattering to be flirted with." She stopped and studied his face. "But maybe I should apologize to you."

"For what?"

"You're white as a ghost."

"And you're enjoying that quite a bit, aren't you?"

"Yes."

She pushed away the plate with food still on it. Either she was finally full or had suddenly lost her appetite. "But I should have said something sooner. It's been a long day and coming home is hard."

"Oh?"

"My great-grandfather has dementia. And my family is kind of upset that I haven't been back to visit him in a while."

"I'm sorry."

"Thank you. And today I found out that said great-grandfather, Josiah Abernathy, had a baby out of wedlock and no one in my family knew about it."

He wasn't sure about turning white when she pointed out her pregnancy, but he felt the color drain from his face now. This was a bad time to find out he never got her last name before bad-mouthing her family. "You're an Abernathy?"

"Guilty." She put her hand on his arm, a consoling gesture. "Don't feel bad. I didn't take it the wrong way. I understand where you're coming from. People in this town don't deal well with change. And my parents are no exception. They respect tradition, passing land down to their children."

"Like I said. We're new money."

"Yeah. It kind of makes you an outsider." She looked down at her stomach and sighed. "They also aren't thrilled that their daughter is pregnant and not married. It's been a long time since I lived here, and I feel a lot like an outsider, too."

"What about the baby's father?"

"Don't you start judging me." Her eyes flashed with anger. "It was bad enough coming from my parents and brother, but I barely know you."

"I wasn't judging," he assured her. "And we just met, but we've shared a lot of information over potato skins and beer."

"Technically, and for the record, I'm drinking club soda with lime."

"That doesn't change the fact that we've bonded over being outsiders."

She thought about that for a moment, then nodded. "Okay. You win. We've bonded."

It was nice to have a friendly conversation with someone. Morgan was just about to ask for her phone number when he saw her expression change. He hadn't known her long but would swear her guard went up. He glanced over his shoulder and saw Gabe Abernathy and Melanie Driscoll walking toward them. Morgan had run into him in town, at events, and the man had been cordial but not overly friendly.

Looking wary, he stopped beside his sister. "Are you okay, Erica?"

"Of course. Why wouldn't I be?"

"Mel and I didn't mean to be gone so long. We ran into some friends and got to talking." He gave Morgan another careful look. "I'm sorry we left you alone."

"It's okay. Morgan kept me company." She looked back and forth between them. "Have you two met?"

"Yes," Gabe said in his best "don't get any ideas" tone.

Erica's eyes narrowed as she looked at her

brother's fiancée. "Mel, you're pretty new in town, aren't you?"

"Yes. And I love it here," she said, as chipper as could be. "People have been so friendly and welcoming."

"I guess that happens when you're engaged to an Abernathy." Morgan maintained a friendly tone, but never looked away from the other man.

"It helps," Gabe said. Then he looked at his sister. "We're leaving. Are you ready to go?"

"Yeah. I'm tired. It's been a long day." From her perch on the high bar stool, she looked hesitantly at the floor. "I just have to get down from here first."

Instantly Morgan got up and took her arms to help her down. Touching her seemed to short-circuit his brain, because he couldn't stop looking at her mouth. With an effort he pulled himself together and said, "Gracefully done."

"Thanks to you." She gave him a grateful look. "It was really nice to meet you, Morgan."

"The pleasure was mine." And he sincerely meant that.

"Good night," Mel said. "I'll see you around, Morgan."

"You will."

Then he watched the three of them walk away. Mostly he watched Erica. From this view it was impossible to tell she was pregnant. She had on leggings and cowboy boots with a sweater covering her hips and butt. What he could see was damn shapely, and her face and smile would steal a man's heart and have him grateful for it.

That's when he remembered he hadn't gotten her phone number. Now that he could think straight again, he realized how idiotic the thought was. Why would he even consider it? But he knew the answer to that. He felt comfortable with her, and that hadn't happened to him in a long time. Clearly she wasn't looking for a relationship but that could be *why* he felt so comfortable with her. He wasn't looking for a relationship either. He'd fallen half in love with Erica Abernathy before realizing she was going to have a baby. And that complicated things in a way that would keep him from making a romantic fool of himself.

The next morning Erica was in the best mood. A man had flirted with her! Granted, when he started, he didn't know she was pregnant. What pleased and surprised her the most was that he didn't seem to lose interest when he found out.

Another surprise was how nice it felt waking up in her old room. Her mom kept it the way it was when Erica left for college. She slept in her queen-size bed with the brass headboard. Across from it was a cherrywood dresser and matching dressing table where she did her makeup. Lace curtains crisscrossed the window that had a spectacular view of the mountains. The walls were painted a pale lavender, with white doors and trim. And the room came with an en suite bathroom. The whole effect was soothing.

Except for the part where she couldn't get last night out of her mind. A man like that—those shoulders, that voice and face. His blue eyes twinkled with humor and he was tan, evidence of a rugged outdoor life. And he admitted flirting with her and wanting her phone number. In an alternate universe, where she wasn't pregnant and as big as the *Queen Mary*, she'd have seriously flirted back.

So it was probably a good thing she had her own personal speed bump. After being dumped by the man she'd thought was The One, then watching him take up with another woman so soon after, her self-esteem had been pretty battered. Last night made her feel better.

After showering, then doing her hair and makeup, she slipped on a dress she hoped projected confident professionalism. Then she went downstairs.

Erica heard voices, which was unusual at this hour. She'd only expected to see her mother, as her father was almost always busy with ranch work by now. Not today. And she got a bonus surprise. Her brother, Gabe, was there, too. And Grandpa Alexander. She kissed his cheek and gave him a hug.

"It's good to see you, Erica." The silver-haired man smiled, but there were questions in his eyes.

"How come you guys aren't out working?" She

was practically positive the four of them had been talking about her, because they clammed up when she'd walked into the room. Now they all looked guilty. "What?"

"Good morning, sweetie." Her mother set the spatula she'd been holding on the granite countertop beside the stainless steel stove. "Did you sleep well?"

"As well as can be expected, what with being as big as a house." She made eye contact with each one of them. "Don't let me interrupt. Feel free to continue talking about me."

Gabe snorted. "What makes you think we were talking about you?"

"Oh please." She put a hand on her hip. "Since when are you and Daddy and Grandpa not doing ranch chores at this time of day? I grew up hearing that there's always something to be done around here. This looks very much like a family meeting. And it's not a leap to figure out that I'm the topic of discussion, since my presence on the Ambling A is the only variable."

"Why don't you let me make you a plate of food?" her mother suggested. "You need to keep up your strength."

"Thank you, Mama. Something smells wonderful. But first I'd like to know what's going on." She looked at her brother pointedly, and he squirmed under her gaze.

"You know I've always had your best interests at heart," he started.

"That's how you start when someone isn't going to like what you're about to say. Does this have anything to do with last night at DJ's?"

He pressed his lips together and wouldn't quite meet her gaze, confirming the theory. "Do you always chat up strangers at a bar, sis?"

"Obviously you're talking about Morgan Dalton." Just saying his name brought to mind a very appealing image of the man, and it made her tummy flutter. This was something she hadn't felt in a long time. Or maybe ever. "He seemed to be a very nice man. I liked him a lot."

"Looks can be deceiving," her mother said.

"Do you have something against him?" Erica asked the question and looked at all of them for a response.

"The Daltons are new to Bronco Heights," Grandpa Alexander said.

"No one knows much about them." Her father planted his feet wide apart and folded his arms over his chest.

She remembered what Morgan had said about local folks being a little standoffish.

"Has anyone bothered to get to know them?" she demanded.

"There are rumors. You know how this town is." Her mother didn't actually answer the question.

"Mel's friend Amanda is engaged to his brother. I heard something about the father cheating on his wife. No one knows how they got the money to buy the ranch."

"If it wasn't legal, I'm sure someone would be in jail." Erica wasn't sure why, but she felt strongly about defending Morgan. She met her brother's gaze. "Does Mel think her friend is making a mistake marrying Morgan's brother?"

Gabe shifted his feet before meeting her gaze. "She said he's a good man and a terrific father."

"Well, what do you know?" Erica looked at each of them in turn. "Amanda found out that one of the Daltons is a stand-up guy because she got to know him."

"People change," Erica continued. "They mature. Let them screw up first before you put their picture on a Most Wanted poster at the post office."

"But, sweetie, you're pregnant," her mother said.

"Not a news flash, Mama."

"He's after something," her father declared.

"Not my money." She was unemployed and her savings wouldn't last long. "I don't have any."

"But your family does." It seemed her father had already made up his mind.

"His ranch seems to be doing fine, no?" she asked them.

"No one knows for sure," Gabe said. "The smart move would be to stay away from him."

Erica looked from her brother to her father to her grandfather. "You know, I find this overprotective streak of yours equal parts adorable and annoying. You do realize that for the past twelve years I've been taking pretty good care of myself."

"Except for the part where you're having a baby without a husband." Her mother didn't pull any punches.

The zinger hit its mark, and Erica heard the message loud and clear. "Thank you all for your advice and I know it comes from a place of caring about me." It was also worth what she'd paid for it, no matter their good intentions. Wasn't the road to hell paved with them? "I'm not very hungry after all, Mama. And I have to run. I have an appointment in town with an attorney."

"Could you do me a favor since you're going into town?" her father asked. "I called in an order to the building supply store. It will fit in your SUV and you be sure to have one of the guys there load it up for you. That would save me a trip. Since I'm behind on work today..."

Because he'd felt an obligation to warn her away from Morgan. Defensiveness didn't trump her sense of obligation to do as he'd asked. "Not a problem, Daddy."

Erica walked away before anyone, including herself, could say another word. She'd grab something to eat before her appointment. More than one friend

in Denver had suggested she might have a case to
sue Barron Enterprises for wrongful termination, so
she'd made the appointment before moving home.

After stopping for a fast-food breakfast sandwich,
she was early for her ten o'clock slot at Randall &
Randall, attorneys at law. It was a brother-sister firm
located in the Bronco Heights business district. The
receptionist was somewhere in her fifties, with
stylishly cut short brown hair and brown eyes. The
nameplate on her desk read Mrs. Frances Randall.
All in the family, Erica thought.

She introduced herself and was politely asked to
take a seat in the expensively furnished waiting area.
Charlotte Randall would be with her shortly.

"Can I get you anything?" Mrs. Randall asked.
"Water? Coffee?"

"Nothing, thanks."

A few minutes later a pretty young woman with
red hair and brown eyes opened the door to the back
offices. "You must be Erica Abernathy. I'm Charlotte
Randall. It's nice to meet you."

"Likewise." Erica stood and shook hands.

"Let's go to my office and you can tell me why
you're here."

They walked down a hall, then turned right into
a large room with a desk full of files and a laptop
buried in the middle of it. Floor-to-ceiling windows
looked out on the gorgeous mountains while diplo-

mas and certificates hanging on the wall proudly displayed her impressive credentials.

Charlotte sat behind the desk. "How can I help you?"

"I'm not sure you can, actually." She took a deep breath. "Until recently I worked for Barron Enterprises in Denver."

"I've heard of it. Big media company headquartered there. Powerful."

"Yeah." Erica fully expected to be told there was no point in wasting time because Barron had an army of lawyers. They would fight any settlement by every legal means necessary and drag out a lawsuit, making it too expensive to continue. "I was fired."

The young woman nodded thoughtfully. "Colorado is an at-will state. That means either an employer or employee can terminate an employment situation at any time without consequences."

"So, you're saying I have no recourse?" Though it was expected, her heart fell. She could practically hear the thud.

"Not necessarily. Were you given a reason for the dismissal?"

"No." She thought for a moment. "I was called in to see the company president. He told me I was being transferred to the Miami office."

Erica went on from there, explaining everything. Dating the boss's son. Their breakup. His relationship with another company employee. "I wanted to quit even before I was called on the carpet."

"Why is that?"

"Peter and that employee's sudden marriage and baby announcement. After that his wife became increasingly hostile as my pregnancy began to show."

"It's a good thing you toughed it out. If you'd quit, you would have lost any standing in the court to file a lawsuit."

"The transfer came out of the blue and I'm in my third trimester. The job I had was traditionally done from the home office in Denver. I pushed back. My boss got angry and said I was fired."

"I see." Charlotte's eyes narrowed a little dangerously. "So there was no misconduct on your part? No job performance issues like habitual tardiness?"

"No. I'd been with the company for eight years and had a spotless record. In fact, before the work environment turned hostile, I was promoted to chief administrative officer."

Charlotte nodded, her expression reflecting respect for that higher management job. "So you want to sue Barron for wrongful termination."

"I believe I was unfairly let go. And that I'm entitled to a severance package at the very least. But you should be aware that my resources are limited, especially because of my pregnancy."

The lawyer smiled. "Frankly, that's what gives you cause to bring suit."

"How so?"

"Even in an at-will state there are exceptions to the rule and legal remedies that could help keep your job, if you still want it. Or go for a settlement because you were wrongfully terminated. One of those exceptions is discrimination for a number of reasons, one of them being pregnancy."

"But I don't think he fired me because I'm having a baby. Everyone knows it's not his son's. It's all about the new wife not wanting to look at me every day and be reminded I dated her husband first." What she kept to herself was that he hadn't wanted to have a baby with Erica.

"It doesn't matter what the motivation for termination was. You're in a protected class and that gives you a very good chance of winning a settlement. No matter how many lawyers the company has. And I don't think they can drag it out. The optics for a powerful media company bullying a pregnant woman are really bad. They know it, and we can use that to pressure them."

"Does that mean you'll take my case?"

"Yes." Charlotte explained that she would take it on contingency and how the attorney-client contract worked. She seemed really eager to get started. "There are laws against what they did to you, Erica. I'll put the paperwork together and have them served as soon as possible."

"Thank you, Charlotte. You have no idea how relieved I am."

Erica left the lawyer's office feeling pretty darn positive. Kind of the way she'd left DJ's last night after Morgan had said *Where have you been all my life*. The memory made her smile, but she also felt a little wistful. In her car behind the steering wheel, she looked down at the belly that prevented her from seeing her feet. She was officially a package deal, and no man in his right mind would want her.

She'd been resigned to that when she decided to take the journey to motherhood alone. But that was before she met Morgan.

It was a short drive to the building supply store. She got out of the car and walked into the cavernous interior guaranteed to make men quiver with excitement. But she was the one doing the quivering when she practically ran into Morgan Dalton standing just inside the door.

Chapter Three

Morgan had been thinking about Erica a lot since last night, but he hadn't expected to see her again. On top of that, the building supply store in town was probably the last place he would have expected to bump into her. Yet here she was. And when she smiled her beautiful smile at him, his day got a whole lot brighter. Possibly because he felt that lightning bolt to the heart even stronger than he had the first time he saw her.

"If it isn't the prettiest pregnant lady in town." Darned if she didn't blush, he thought. If she had at DJ's, the dim lighting in the restaurant prevented him from seeing. She was even more beautiful than she'd been last night, classy and stylish in her gray dress and black boots. Again his gaze was drawn to her full, sexy lips.

"I bet you say that to all the pregnant ladies."

"Nope. As a matter of fact, you're the only one I know." He steered her to the side of the doorway and out of the heavy foot traffic where she might get run into. Reluctantly, he removed his hand from her arm but couldn't stop the tingling in his fingers—or the urge to touch her and never stop. "To what do I owe the good fortune of seeing you again so soon?"

"Actually you can thank my father. I'm picking up an order for him." There was a wry expression on her face and more than a little satisfaction in her smile. "What brings you here?"

"Fencing materials. It's getting to be time to check them out and make repairs. Need to have all the supplies when that chore gets put on the schedule." When that happened, he was pretty sure his father would tag along and continue trying to "mend fences" with him. Morgan would have thought that pun was funny if it was anyone but his dad. He wasn't laughing.

"You turned very serious about something all of a sudden." That statement put a curious look on her face. "Does it have anything to do with family?"

"Why do you ask?"

"Because nine times out of ten a man looking like you do right now is having woman or family trouble.

Since you flirted with me outrageously last night, I don't think it's about a lady. That leaves family. And I have to tell you, there are rumors spreading about yours."

Folks around here hadn't given him an especially warm welcome so he was a little surprised they'd waste their breath gossiping about his family. "I don't know whether to be pissed off or proud."

"Maybe both. But one of the things they're talking about is your brother."

"I've got four," he said. "Still, my guess would be that it's Holt."

Absently she tucked a silky blond strand of hair behind her ear. "Gabe mentioned he's a good man and father."

"Yeah. He is. Ten years ago he had a brush with the law. He did community service, but there's nothing permanent on his record."

"Then that's not a rumor. It's fact."

She wasn't judging, Morgan realized, and liked her even better for it. "Holt isn't proud of it and in a lot of ways that shaped the dad he's become."

"That would make you an uncle. Niece or nephew?" Interest sparked in her hazel eyes, cranking up the green, toning down the brown.

"Nephew. Robby. He's seven. As a matter of fact, somehow my brother talked me into looking after him this afternoon. I'm taking him to Happy Hearts after school."

"I'm sorry. Happy Hearts?"

He laughed at the puzzled expression on her face. "I forgot you just came back. It's an animal sanctuary run by Daphne Taylor. Robby picked out a dog and cat from there, both rescues."

"I know Daphne. She was a year ahead of me in high school." She tapped her lip thoughtfully. "As a matter of fact, I dated her older brother Jordan for a short time the summer after I graduated. He was an older man and I was flattered by the attention. At first."

"Oh?" Jealousy pricked him a little, and that was just plain stupid. Why the hell was it any skin off his nose that she went out with the son of the richest man in town a lot of years ago? And obviously she'd been with someone since then or she wouldn't be pregnant. If, and that was a very big if, there was any skin coming off his nose about anything, it would be that.

"Yeah. I haven't thought about him for a long time. Seems like a lifetime ago." She met his gaze. "My parents made no secret of the fact that they really wanted me to marry Jordan. Partly so I wouldn't go out of state to college."

"But you didn't do that."

"Nope. There was no spark with him." She shrugged.

Damn sparks were sure inconvenient. He was pretty sure he had some for her because he was unreasonably glad she hadn't felt them for Jordan Taylor. "So, are you and Daphne friends?"

"We used to be."

"Then you should come out to the sanctuary. This afternoon maybe. If you don't have something going on."

"I don't."

"You could meet Robby. See your friend." *I could see you.*

"Maybe." She nodded thoughtfully. "Now I better see about my father's order."

"Yeah. And I have to get those supplies."

It turned out the order for her father was wood cut into short pieces and a couple bags of hardware that were already loaded onto a cart. One of the store employees started to wheel it out to her SUV in the parking lot, but Morgan offered to help.

He followed her to the car and put her rear passenger seat down flat, then slid the boards in one by one. That gave him the chance to spend a couple more minutes with her. Just in case he didn't see her later. On a one to ten stupid scale, that probably earned him a twenty.

Erica drove back to the Ambling A feeling as if she'd been on an emotional roller coaster all day. She woke up in a great mood but her family managed to bring her down with warnings to steer clear of Morgan Dalton. Then the lawyer said she had a strong case for a settlement and while doing her dad a favor she ran into Morgan.

When she saw him, she got that shivery feeling in the pit of her stomach again. The same thing she'd felt at DJ's, only stronger, especially because he kept looking at her mouth. He didn't have to mention the outing with his nephew, but he had. And, doggone it, she was curious to see him with a seven-year-old boy. Then she factored in her family's advice, the same family she was trying to make peace with.

It might be best to avoid Morgan. Not because she believed he wasn't a decent person, but because every instinct said he was. He seemed like an awfully nice man. And he was hot. In a world where she wasn't pregnant there was a good chance she'd have kissed him when he looked at her mouth. But she was pregnant, so that was that.

She drove down the long road to the ranch, turned toward the outbuildings and corral, then parked by the barn. Her father had said he would be there most of the day. She sniffed the air and savored the familiar, earthy scent of animals and hay. She'd forgotten how pleasant this all was. And inside the barn it was even stronger as she walked through. She located her dad in the tack room sitting on a stool in front of the workbench.

"Daddy, I've got the stuff you ordered from the building supply store."

"Thanks." He glanced over his shoulder. "I'll come unload it."

"Okay."

He slid off the wooden stool and walked toward her, a frown on his face. "Who loaded the car for you? Was it Jerry?"

She debated the pros and cons of telling him who had. In the end, she couldn't resist messing with him. After all, he'd warned her off Morgan, then sent her on an errand where he happened to be. Karma was funny that way. "No, I didn't lift a finger. Jerry offered, but Morgan Dalton happened to be there and he helped me out."

"Hmm." That was his only comment.

But Erica could feel the tension from him crank up. She didn't like this awkwardness and needed to try and lighten things up. She followed him out to her car, where he lifted the tailgate and pulled out a couple pieces of the wood.

"What are you going to do with this?" she asked.

"I'm building something."

"What?" she asked.

"A piece of furniture," he said vaguely.

"Something for Mama?"

"Sort of."

She walked after him back through the barn to the tack room but he didn't elaborate.

"I have a lot of good memories growing up here with Grandpa Alex and Gramps."

"Is that so?" Her dad set down the boards in an empty space on the far wall. He pulled his Stetson a little lower on his forehead. "Funny, you didn't have any trouble walking away."

It was on the tip of her tongue to explain her reasons again. How she wanted independence. And didn't want to be pressured into marrying Jordan. Or settling down in Bronco, Montana without ever experiencing another way of life. But she kept that to herself because this man had heard it all before and none of what she'd said changed his attitude.

"Do you remember that litter of kittens the barn cat had?"

"Yup." He walked past her back outside.

Erica followed behind him, just like when she was a little girl and shadowed him everywhere. "They were so cute."

"Took us forever to get rid of 'em."

"You mean find them good homes."

"Whatever," he said.

"Morgan told me about Happy Hearts, the animal sanctuary. His nephew adopted a dog and cat. If that place had been around, we wouldn't have had such a hard time getting people to take the kittens."

"Hmm." He set a few more boards down with the others, then turned to make another trip.

"I'll never forget that time we went fishing in the creek. You were trying to teach me how to cast a line."

"And you fell in." He half smiled. "Your mama wasn't too happy with us."

"No, she wasn't." As they walked through the barn, she saw the stall where her first horse had lived. "Do you remember Belle?"

"Of course. You learned to ride on her."

"Yeah." She fell off and broke her arm, too. But she was trying to lighten his mood, not remind him how he blamed himself for that accident. "She was a sweetheart."

"Gramps knew she would be. He picked her out for you."

Erica had forgotten that. Again she felt bad about not seeing him more while she could still talk to him about these memories.

"Gabe told me about the baby girl Gramps gave up for adoption. Beatrix."

"Yeah." Her father put the last piece of wood on the stack.

"He and Mel are trying to find her. Do you think they will?"

"Long shot, I figure."

"She would be your—" Erica did the family connection in her head "—aunt. How do you feel about all this?"

"Family is family. It's good to know your folks, I guess. For us and for her."

"Yes." Erica sat on the stool while he went to get the bags of hardware. When he came back she said,

"It's weird to think about Gramps having a baby and not telling anyone."

Her father's gaze snapped to hers, and irony glittered in his hazel eyes. "You didn't tell any of us you were going to have a baby until yesterday. And only because you had to."

"I would have said something. Eventually," she mumbled. This was not going at all as she'd hoped. Instead of easing the tension between them, she was making it worse.

"I don't understand this world anymore," he said. "Times are changing. I can't keep up. And not sure I want to."

"Talk to me, Daddy." That was the most he'd said. Maybe he was ready to get it out in the open. "What's bugging you?"

His gaze settled on her belly for several moments, so she braced herself for more third degree about the baby's father. When he finally spoke, she was surprised by what he said.

"You really want to know what's got me twisted up?" He set the bag down. "That damn animal sanctuary of Daphne Taylor's."

"What?" Her eyes opened wider. "Why?"

"This is cattle country. It's always been survival of the fittest. That's nature's way. What doesn't kill you makes you stronger. That's a cliché now, but it's always been the way of it on a ranch. Whether it's horses or cows, the ones that make it against the odds ensure the strength of the bloodlines to produce hardy offspring able to withstand adverse conditions. Like cold, heat, drought and anything else Mother Nature throws at us."

Erica could understand his point of view, but science made advances to benefit animals and humans. Without artificial insemination she wouldn't be having this baby. Those words would not come out of her mouth, however. Her father would never understand how very much she wanted this child. How deeply she'd longed to be a mother.

"Look at it this way, Daddy. As I understand it, Daphne takes in animals and hooks them up with someone to love them. Like an adoption agency." Or a sperm bank. "She provides a service to the community."

"If you ask me, that girl has too much time on her hands if she can take care of animals that have no practical function."

"You have dogs," she pointed out. "And you love them."

"I do. But they serve a purpose on this ranch. They herd cattle."

"Okay." Time to exit this conversation. "Just so I'm clear. Does this mean you're a no vote on Happy Hearts?"

For half a second he grinned, as if forgetting to be mad at her. As if she was the smart-ass kid he'd always called her. Then the amusement disappeared and serious dad was back.

"Have you ever seen this animal place?" he asked. "After all, you've been gone for twelve years."

She refused to engage on something she couldn't change. "No, I haven't been there yet."

"Okay, then." That meant *don't argue something you know nothing about*. He pointed to the bench where the tack was laid out. "I've got work to do."

"Right." She slid off the stool and moved toward the doorway.

"Erica?"

"Hmm?" She turned back toward him.

"How did your appointment go? With the lawyer?"

"Oh." She'd almost forgotten. "She said I have a strong case and will draw up the paperwork to file the lawsuit."

"Good. Thanks for getting my order." He nodded and picked up a bridle, effectively turning his back on her and any more conversation.

"You're welcome. See you later."

She headed outside, mulling over their talk. One positive thing had come out of it, and her dad wouldn't like the result. He was right that she was advocating for something she knew nothing about. So, she made up her mind to go to the animal sanctuary. She smiled when she realized the trip came with a bonus. Morgan would be there with his nephew.

* * *

Morgan finished feeding the horses, then jumped in his truck for the short drive to his house on Dalton's Grange. It was one of three, the other two going to the second- and third-oldest Dalton brothers— Holt and Boone.

His place had three bedrooms, two baths, living and dining rooms and a kitchen. A little more space than a single cowboy needed and this was the second largest. They'd agreed Holt should have the most square footage since he had a boy he was raising.

That boy was the reason he was in such a hurry. He was going to pick up Robby from school, then take him to Happy Hearts. While Holt was attending a cattlemen's association meeting, his fiancée, Amanda, had promised the kid an outing. Morgan was going along to provide another pair of eyes, or possibly some muscle. Robby loved to roam and roughhouse. And if Erica showed up while they were there, well, he sure as heck wouldn't turn down another chance to hang out with her.

Fifteen minutes later he was showered, changed into clean clothes and smelled pretty good, too. There was a knock on his door, and when he opened it, Holt and Amanda were there. She was a pretty little thing with long brown hair and eyes the color of warm chocolate.

He hugged her. "Hey. When are you going to get smart and leave this guy to run away with me?"

She laughed. "As tempting as that offer is, I love him."

"Hands off my woman, big brother." Holt didn't look the least bit worried. He'd loved her for a long time, and they were eager to be a family for his son.

Morgan was teasing, but if he did have a thing for her, he'd fight it into submission. No way he'd be like his father and cross the boundaries of fidelity. But he had to ask, "How come you don't think I could take her away from you?"

"Because with women you're all hat and no saddle. As soon as one gets seriously sweet on you, that's it. You're outta there." Holt grinned. "You're only interested when there's no serious danger of making a commitment."

Morgan admitted, if only to himself, that his brother had a point. But he was a little envious of Holt's happiness. "How did you guys know you were it for each other?"

"That's hard to put into words." Holt thought for a moment. "The first time I laid eyes on Amanda, I knew she was something special." He smiled down at her. "That was ten years ago. It didn't work out then, but I never forgot her. And now she's never getting rid of me."

"As if." She moved closer and slid her arm around his waist. "To answer your question, Morgan, love is when you light up in the presence of one certain person. That someone you can't wait to be with and never want to leave. It can sneak up on you gradually or hit you like a bolt of lightning. And you just *know*."

He doubted he'd find that, but out loud he teased, "That's the best you can do?"

She shook her head, exasperated. "You're impossible."

"Thank you. I try."

"And succeed nicely," Holt joked. "Seriously, Morgan, thanks for helping out with Robby today. He's always pretty active but after being cooped up in school all day he'll have a lot of energy to work off."

"Happy to help." Morgan had a deep respect for his brother, raising his son alone for the last four years. The boy's mother hadn't wanted to be a mom but Holt handled fatherhood like a pro, better than anyone could have imagined. "How did you get to be such a good dad? God knows ours left a lot to be desired in the role model department."

"Neal isn't as bad as you make him out. He's made mistakes, but he loves our mom. When she was in the hospital after the heart attack, I overheard him talking to the chaplain, promising to be a better husband. I believe he was sincere," Holt said. "And don't sell yourself short, big brother. You're really good with my kid. Just saying."

"Glad you think so."

"I know so. You are and always were a great big

brother, looking out for the rest of us. And, except for Amanda, I trust you with my son more than anyone."

"Stop," Morgan teased. "You'll make me blush, or cry. Or both."

Holt grinned. "Robby will cry if you guys are late and he's waiting in front of the school all alone."

"Let's go get him, then."

Holt kissed Amanda, then said, "I'm off to my meeting. Be home as soon as I can."

They walked outside, and before getting in his truck, Holt kissed Amanda one more time as if he didn't want to let her go. After he drove away, she and Morgan got into his truck and headed out to pick up his nephew.

When the boy was successfully retrieved from school and in the truck, Morgan thanked the good Lord for booster seats and seat belts that kept an active boy contained. It did not, however, put any limitations on the chatter. All the way there the kid talked about Bentley and Oliver, the dog and cat he'd brought home from the sanctuary.

He made the turn onto the road leading to the facility. There were two buildings—a barn and a squat structure for the smaller animals. In an enclosure, he could see goats, pigs and a variety of creatures milling around.

When Morgan parked the truck in the dirt lot, Amanda said so only he could hear, "I'm under strict orders *not* to let him get attached to an animal or under any circumstances bring another one home."

"Okay." Morgan scanned the open area and was disappointed when he spotted a few trucks and cars but no SUV with Colorado license plates.

"Is something wrong?" she asked.

"Hmm? What?" He met her gaze. "No. All good."

"Yay, we're here," Robby shouted. "I'm going to see Tiny Tim."

"That potbellied pig is his favorite," Amanda said.

"No kidding. If we brought it home, do you think Holt would ever trust me with his son again?" he teased. Then he gave the area one more look for the familiar car.

"In a word? No." She laughed, but it faded when she studied him. "Are you looking for someone?"

"No." Yes, he thought. Until he didn't see Erica, he realized just how very much he'd been looking forward to it. "Why do you ask?"

"You look like that potbellied pig just two-stepped all over your favorite Stetson."

"No. I'm good." The rear passenger door slammed shut, a clue Robby had freed himself and was off. "And we're up."

"Right."

Morgan slid out of the truck and called after his nephew. "Stay where we can see you."

"Okay, Uncle Morgan." But he continued to race

toward the animal enclosure as fast as those seven-year-old legs could go.

Amanda came around the truck and stood beside him, shading her eyes from the sun with her hand. "He'll be fine. Daphne is out there with the animals. She'll look out for him."

Behind them there was the sound of a car driving up the road. Dust trailed behind it, but the SUV looked familiar. It was the same color as Erica's, and he smiled. Although he didn't realize he was until Amanda pointed it out.

"Someone you know?" It was the tone a woman used when she knew the answer to her own question and planned to make something of it.

"Yeah. Erica Abernathy."

"And you know her—how?"

"Ran into her last night at DJ's then again today at the building supply store." With everything he had, he was trying to look indifferent.

"Well, you're lighting up, Morgan." She was definitely making this into something. "Did she know you were coming out here?"

"I might have mentioned we'd be here this afternoon."

"Hmm."

Morgan had no idea what that meant. Could be anything from "she's way out of your league" to "I can tell you're sweet on her." Oddly, he wanted both of those things to be true.

The SUV parked next to them and two women exited. Erica had brought Melanie with her.

"Mel!" Amanda squealed with delight when she saw her friend and gave her a hug.

"Hi." Erica walked around the front of her car and smiled at him, then the other two women. "I found her wandering around the Ambling A, and she had the day off. She volunteered to show me where she adopted her cat."

"Where are my manners?" Mel said. "Erica, this is my friend Amanda Jenkins. We met when I rented an apartment in the same complex as Amanda and her roommate Brittany." She looked at her friend. "This is Gabe's sister. She just came in from Colorado."

"Nice to meet you, Erica." Amanda said to both women, "I guess you know Morgan Dalton."

"Yes. He helped me out today," Erica said. "Loaded some stuff in my car."

"Aren't you the gallant one." Amanda had a shrewd expression on her face that implied she could read his mind and thought he was an idiot for trying to pretend indifference.

"Speaking of Brittany, I sure haven't seen much of her lately," Mel said. "I get short phone calls and texts. Reading between the lines, she couldn't be happier." She turned to Erica and explained, "Brittany's married to Daniel Dubois, a local rancher who's raising his orphaned niece." Then she turned her attention back to Mel. "I hear she's up to her ears in alligators what with handling Denim and Diamonds."

"What's Denim and Diamonds?" Erica asked.

"It's a black tie fundraiser," Amanda explained, then mentioned the early November date. "It's going to be a real swanky affair at the Taylor Ranch. Everyone is going to be there. You should come, Erica."

"Oh, I don't know—"

"Your folks are probably going. Gabe is too, right, Mel?"

"We wouldn't miss it," she agreed.

Erica looked down at her gently rounded belly. "Only two problems. It's the week before my due date. So…"

"I don't see that as an issue if you haven't had the baby yet." Amanda shrugged.

"You said two problems," Morgan reminded her. "What's the second one?"

She looked up at him and tucked a strand of blond hair behind her ear when it blew across her lips. After hesitating a fraction of a second, she said, "Remember I told you I dated Jordan Taylor a long time ago?"

"Yeah." How could he forget? His reaction to it was way out of proportion. But the other two women looked pretty surprised at her revelation.

"Well," Erica continued, "I met his father. Cornelius. Just a couple of times but he was always bossy and domineering. Going to any event on his ranch makes me a little uncomfortable."

"There will be so many people there he probably won't even see you," Melanie said.

"I'll be even bigger by then. No one will be able to miss me."

"You are not that big," Amanda assured her. "And we just met, so if this is out of line, don't judge. But it looks as if pregnancy agrees with you. You're radiant."

Morgan couldn't agree more, but kept that to himself. No way a guy should insert himself into this conversation. Although he could see a vulnerability in Erica that made him feel protective.

"Thanks." Erica smiled a little shyly, a lot self-consciously. "I appreciate that. And just so you know, I wasn't fishing for compliments."

"I didn't think you were." Amanda waved it off. "And you really should think about coming. It will be the biggest social event of the year. From what Brittany says, the guest list is pretty extensive. You're going, right, Morgan?"

His father mentioned an invitation and Neal Dalton had said it was a good chance to expand their ties to the community. He wanted the whole family to show up and their mother agreed with him. Morgan and his brothers would do anything for her, so that pretty much made it a command appearance.

"I wish I could say no, but…"

"So you'll see some friendly faces, Erica," Amanda persisted.

"Still," she said hesitantly, "Jordan's father can be intimidating. Facing him alone—"

"I'll go with you." Morgan was just as surprised as the three women when the words came out of his mouth.

Chapter Four

Erica held her breath, expecting any second for Morgan to grin at her and say *Gotcha*. Or *Just kidding*. She couldn't believe he'd just volunteered to escort her to the biggest social event of the year. But he looked completely serious and possibly a little embarrassed. Mel and Amanda were staring at both of them, and she couldn't imagine what they must be thinking. Actually she could see that her brother's fiancée was a little shocked—maybe even a little skeptical.

"That's awfully brave of you to offer," Erica finally said.

"Why?" He shrugged. "I don't mind running interference for you. And you'd be doing me a favor. If I have to go, the least you could do is go with me so I have someone to talk to."

"But I'm pregnant." *Nothing like stating the obvious, but... Seriously?*

"Really? I didn't notice," he teased.

"I'm not even sure I'll go." Erica looked at the two women who'd been glancing back and forth between them, like watching a tennis match.

"It's over a month away," Amanda said. "There's time to decide."

"That's true," Mel agreed a little too quickly. "Talk about it later. We came here to see the farm animals. I was going to show you around, remember?"

"And I have to go make sure Robby isn't driving Daphne crazy." Amanda headed for the farm buildings. "Mel, why don't you come with me and say hi to Daphne. There might be another cat adoption in your future."

"No more for me. But I love looking at the kittens." She glanced over her shoulder. "Coming, Erica?"

"I'm right behind you. Moving a little slowly these days."

"Okay." Mel nodded and hurried after her friend.

When they were alone, Erica turned to Morgan. "Seriously? You asked me on a date?"

"I wasn't thinking about that so much as offering

moral support. And I wasn't kidding about having someone to talk to."

"I'm not all that sure I *want* to talk to anyone at a big posh party."

They started slowly walking toward the two buildings. Robby had disappeared inside the smaller one, and she saw Mel and Amanda go in there, too. Chickens wandered everywhere, pecking at the dirt, while ducks waddled aimlessly. Goats moved around the enclosure and made bleating sounds.

"Why wouldn't you? Want to talk to anyone, I mean?" Morgan asked. "You grew up around here. Aren't there people you want to reconnect with?"

"Not right now. There's no way to hide my belly, and everyone will be curious and it's none of their business." She looked up at the tall man strolling beside her. "I don't feel like I belong here anymore. That's why I'm not sure if I even want to go."

"Okay, then. To be continued."

His black Stetson shaded his eyes, hiding his expression so she couldn't tell what he was thinking. But he must have questions. To his credit, he didn't ask, and that added to his likability points.

As they strolled, their arms bumped and brushed together. He was wearing a fleece-lined jacket against the chill in the air. But every time their bodies connected, even in the slightest way, Erica swore she could see sparks. And there was a definite fluttering in her stomach, an I-really-like-this-guy feeling. And it didn't hurt that he was helping look after his nephew and had brought him to see the animals.

"So, this is quite a place Daphne has here." Erica felt the need to change the subject to something not about a date.

Morgan told her about the glassed-off cat room inside with hay bales where the animals could frolic freely. Across from it, he explained, there was an area for the dogs that had an outside door to a fenced-in area with runs where they could roam at will.

"Before Daphne opened the sanctuary, this property sat empty for a lot of years. There are rumors it's haunted."

"Really?" She felt a shiver, but it had nothing to do with awareness of him and everything to do with being just a little freaked out.

"You never heard that? You used to live here."

"Maybe." Funny how much a woman could forget in the twelve years she'd been away. "Wasn't there a fire here?"

"That's what I've been told." Their shoulders bumped, and he looked down at her, hesitated a moment, then stuck his hands in the pockets of his jacket. As if he needed to do something safe with them. "The story is that when the barn burned down, a cowboy died along with his girlfriend and some horses." They strolled around the enclosure, and goats moved up to the fence, bleating piteously. "Story has it that the ghosts of the cowboy and the woman show up here and sometimes horses are neighing when none are around."

"Nothing creepy about that." She moved a little closer to him. "If your offer about running interference for me still stands, feel free to go for it if the ghosts show up."

"You don't believe in that kind of thing, do you?" He grinned and tipped his head enough to show the amusement in his eyes.

"I'm reserving judgment." Although not on his smile. It rocked her world as surely as if she'd seen a ghost. She felt tingles in places that never tingled before. "Speaking of judgment, my father is not a fan of a farm animal sanctuary."

"Oh?"

"Nope. He thinks farm animals should be able to pull their own weight. Work. Earn their keep and if they can't... well, let nature take its course."

"I'm a rancher, too. I can see his point."

Maybe her father's attitude about Morgan would be more favorable if he knew they shared an opinion. For some reason it mattered whether or not her dad liked the Daltons.

"So you think Daphne has too much time on her hands and should abandon the animals?" Erica asked him.

"I didn't say that. This place is important to Daphne and a lot of other folks, too. She's making it work. Live and let live, I say. But your father and mine are ranchers from a different generation."

"True." She hadn't thought about it like that. And mentioning his father opened the door on their conversation just that morning. "Remember those rumors about your family I mentioned? There were more."

"Such as?"

She wasn't sure but thought he might be trying too hard to cover irritation with nonchalance. She stopped walking and looked at the animals in a cluster close by trying to get their attention. "It was something about your dad cheating on your mom."

His mouth pulled tight for a moment as he stared at the mountains in the distance. "Although I have no clue how that became public knowledge, it's a fact."

"Are your parents still together?"

"Mom forgave him." His tone said he didn't approve. He shook his head. "He swears the women meant nothing. Just slipups when he was drinking and stressed about money."

Erica was a little surprised he admitted that. But maybe he was in the mood to share. "Speaking of money... Where did your dad get the money to buy the ranch? Please tell me you're not a reincarnation of the Dalton Gang from the Old West. They were brothers who specialized in train and bank robberies."

His mouth curved up in a reluctant smile. "Nothing illegal. He won it in Vegas. A three-buck bet on a million-dollar slot machine. On one pull he won a bundle. He sold his ranch and came here for a fresh start."

"Wow." She could feel her eyes widen. "Now you and your brothers are all here."

"For our mom. We were scattered, working ranches all over. She wanted the family together."

"I guess it's a mom thing." Without conscious thought, she put her hands on her baby bump. "It won't be long until I know what that feels like. I have an appointment with a doctor the day after tomorrow."

"Already?"

"Yeah. Because of being fired and having to move home, I had to find a new doctor."

"A lot of change in a short period of time." His rugged face was suddenly creased with concern.

"It is. I really liked my obstetrician. And to start with someone new so close to the end of this pregnancy is a little scary." Erica didn't know why she was confiding all this to Morgan. She liked him and was comfortable with him, had been from the moment they met. On top of that, she didn't feel there was anyone else she could confide in. Lately, she blamed her hormones for everything, so why not blame them for spilling her guts to this man? "The thing is, I have no choice."

"Are you going alone?"

"Yes." She was doing this whole adventure alone. Nothing had changed just because she came home.

"I thought maybe your mom would go with you. Or Mel."

She shrugged. "I don't want to bother my mom. And Mel is busy working."

He stared at her for a long moment and seemed as if he had another question. But what he said instead was a surprise. "I'll go with you to the doctor, if you want."

"Wow." Her heart fluttered a little. "Why? More running interference for me? That's getting to be a thing with you."

"Just moral support." He shrugged. "Doesn't seem right for you to go alone."

Her eyes suddenly grew moist at his sweet offer, proving her hormones were at it again. "That's awfully considerate of you, but I'll be fine by myself."

"Okay."

He opened his mouth, then shut it again. There must be a million questions in his mind but he didn't ask. That made her like him even more than she already did. And she already liked him quite a bit.

Childish laughter floated to them on a light breeze, and Morgan looked at the small animal building. "I better go make sure Amanda doesn't need help with Robby."

"I'm so sorry. I've talked your ear off," she said.

"Can't say you're not a distraction."

A good or bad one, she wondered but couldn't tell from his expression. Now they walked quickly and were just opening the door when, without warning, Robby came running outside, straight into Erica.

She was a little clumsy these days what with her body being out of proportion, and the unexpected bump knocked her back a couple of steps.

Morgan instantly caught her arm to steady her. At the same time he said, "Robby, remember what your dad says about watching where you're going."

"Yes, sir." He looked up and pushed the brown, shaggy hair out of his blue eyes. "Sorry."

"That's okay, kiddo. No harm done." Erica smiled. "You're a very handsome young man."

"Thank you," he said courteously.

"I'm Erica Abernathy."

"Nice to meet you." Apparently that was all the polite a seven-year-old who was quivering with excitement could manage. "I'm gonna look at the horses and cows now."

Morgan followed him and called out over his shoulder, "I'm on it."

Amanda and Melanie emerged from the building with another woman. Erica recognized Daphne Taylor's strawberry blond hair and doe-shaped blue eyes. The recognition was mutual and then those blue eyes took in her pregnancy.

"Oh my God, Erica! Look at you." Her friend moved closer and hugged her. "You're back."

"I am." She glanced around. "And you've got this place."

"I do. It's my pride and joy. And not without controversy." Her eyes narrowed. "My father doesn't approve."

"Neither does mine." Erica put her hands on her pregnant belly.

They smiled over shared paternal disapproval just as Morgan walked out of the barn carrying Robby and scolding.

"You'll get hurt climbing on the stalls like that, buddy. The animals spook and could hurt you without meaning to."

The boy did look remorseful as he rubbed a finger beneath his nose leaving a dirty streak. "I didn't mean to scare 'em."

"I know you didn't."

"If I promise not to scare 'em, can I go see the goats, Uncle Morgan?"

"Yes. But be careful and watch where you are." Morgan easily lowered the boy and his feet were moving before they even touched the ground.

"I've got it this time, Morgan." Amanda followed the boy, and the other two women tagged along.

"He's a cutie," Erica said. "Pretty active boy."

"That kid just took ten years off my life when he fell into the horse's stall." Exasperation laced with fear tightened Morgan's features as he shook his head. "I don't know how my brother does it. Kids.

It's one thing to watch him for an afternoon, but I don't know if I'd want to be responsible for one all the time."

Erica's warm feeling instantly cooled. For reasons she couldn't understand, she suddenly felt lonelier than at any other point on this solo journey to motherhood. When Morgan had offered to accompany her to the doctor, hope must have taken root. The idea of someone to share the experience.

But based on his reaction just now, this man didn't particularly like kids. Her disappointment about that was way out of line. She had no right to be disappointed because that smacked of having expectations of more. Because of the baby, friendship was it for them.

Two days later Erica drove to the Women's Health Center where her new OB was located in the Bronco Heights medical district. The minute she was fired and realized her only option was to move home, she worked on securing a new doctor. With the help of her Denver OB she'd found this new physician, made an appointment and had all her records forwarded even before packing up her apartment.

She pulled up to the parking structure entrance, took a ticket and the gate lifted, allowing her to drive in and look for a space. Nerves tied her stomach in knots because she was so sure she had everything figured out when she'd made her decision to use insemination to have a baby. Changing doctors during this pregnancy hadn't been part of her strategy.

She'd established a bond and trusted her Denver doctor and would barely get to know this one before her baby was born.

She found a parking space on the fifth level, then walked to the elevator. After riding it down to the first floor lobby, she checked the building directory and found Grace Turner, Obstetrics and Gynecology, Suite 100. Right around the corner.

Pressing a hand to her belly, she whispered, "Here we go, little one."

Sliding the strap of her purse more firmly on her shoulder, Erica took a deep breath and walked into the office. She checked in at the reception desk, and after filling out the forms, she looked around the waiting room. A quick glance told her she was the only expectant mother without a partner. She wished she'd accepted Morgan's offer to accompany her and would welcome his way of making her laugh.

The families around her were in different stages of development. The couple by themselves seemed to be expecting their first child and were clearly nervous. A father and mother had a brand-new tiny, adorable baby in a car seat and looked tired. The last couple had a little one running around as they prepared to add another to their growing brood. One by one the expectant moms were called back to see the doctor.

Erica was wistful but would rather do it alone

than not at all. Her first choice was the traditional way but that hadn't worked out. Her next thought was a flashback of Morgan the other day, sounding as if he didn't want any part of fatherhood. Later she'd observed him protecting Robby from overeager baby goats. Tossing the laughing child in the air. Affectionately ruffling the boy's hair. Sure looked as if he was at least a favorite uncle and enjoying the heck out of it.

The door to the back office opened and a woman in pink scrubs stood there. "Erica?"

Immediately she stood and walked over. "That's me."

"Come on back. I'm Scarlett, Dr. Turner's nurse." She closed the door and indicated the scale behind her. "I guess you probably know the drill."

"Yup." She set her purse on the chair beside it and stepped on.

Scarlett made a note, then led the way down a hall and stopped outside the ladies' room. "I guess you know the drill for this, too."

"My favorite thing," Erica joked.

After getting a sample and leaving it where instructed, she met the nurse in the hall and followed her to a room. She sat at the end of a paper-covered exam table and had her blood pressure taken.

"Good." Scarlet recorded the result, then smiled. "The doctor will be in to see you shortly."

"Thank you."

In Denver, Erica had felt just fine waiting by herself in the exam room. What was it about being back home that made her feel more alone? Probably the sad disappointment and regret in her mother's eyes every time she looked at her pregnant belly. Her happy childhood home now wasn't a happy or accepting place to talk about her baby. It always felt as if she was the elephant in the room.

Not long after the nurse left, the door opened and a thirtyish woman walked into the room. Holding out her hand she said, "I'm Dr. Turner. It's nice to meet you, Erica."

"Thank you for fitting me in. I had a change in work status and moved home. It's so late in my pregnancy, and I wasn't sure how that would all fall into place."

"Believe it or not, women change doctors in the third trimester for a lot of reasons." She was a very pretty blue-eyed brunette. "I received your medical records from your previous OB and reviewed them. I saw the early ultrasound and there's a note in your chart that you don't want to know the baby's sex?"

"That's right."

"So you want to be surprised. No gender reveal party?"

"No."

Her close friends were all in Denver. She'd been gone for so long there wasn't anyone here in Bronco she'd want to invite. Maybe Morgan. But she couldn't picture him amid a cloud of pink or blue balloons.

"And this baby was conceived with IUI using donor sperm."

"Yes."

"Okay. Is the baby moving a lot?"

"I think this child is going to be a kickboxer."

Dr. Turner grinned. "That's what I like to hear."

"It's reassuring. Although at two in the morning…"

"That's Mother Nature's way of preparing you for those night feedings." There was a sympathetic look on the doctor's face. "Go ahead and lie back on the table. I want to do a Doppler and measure your abdomen."

After Erica did as instructed, the doctor moved the instrument over her belly. She nodded. "This baby's heartbeat is strong. Everything looks good. And I think pregnancy agrees with you."

"I've never felt better," she said truthfully. "I experienced some morning sickness and was a little tired in the beginning. But now I feel great."

"It shows. I know it's a cliché, but you really are glowing."

"Thank you."

"Do you have any questions for me?" Dr. Turner asked.

"Yes, actually. I was enrolled in a childbirth class but had to withdraw when I moved. Is it too late now to do that?"

"You've got a little over a month. And it's never

too late. The more you know, the better. I can give you some information on a class that's just starting at the Health Center and arrange enrollment if you'd like."

"That would be great."

"Do you have a birthing coach?" The doctor must have seen something in her face because she quickly added, "It can be anyone—a relative or friend."

"What if I don't have one? Can I still take the class?"

"Of course. There's a lot of good information for first-time moms or even a refresher course for women who already have babies. Methods of delivery. How to know when you're in labor. What to do if your water breaks. Relaxation techniques. Pain management options. Breastfeeding. Caring for a newborn."

"Sounds like—pun intended—just what the doctor ordered."

The woman smiled. "Okay. I'll have Scarlett put together the information, and she'll give it to you when you check out."

"I was nervous about this appointment but you've really put me at ease, Doctor."

"Then I've done my job. Just relax and enjoy the rest of your pregnancy," she advised.

That was easy for her to say, Erica thought. The woman didn't have to find a job and a labor coach, not necessarily in that order.

Chapter Five

The Ambling A had a herd bull for sale and Dalton's Grange needed one to improve the calf crop, so Morgan was sitting across a desk from Gabe Abernathy. The main house was pretty impressive and this office kept that theme going. It was filled with rich leather chairs, wood beams overhead and a stone fireplace. The environment smelled of old money and reminded Morgan that until recently his family hadn't had much to spare.

The Abernathys' operation produced superior stock and they'd quickly agreed on a price, making the negotiation smoother than he expected.

"So, we have a deal?" he asked.

"Yes."

"Good." Morgan leaned forward and put out his hand, the way gentlemen did to finalize a negotiation. The other man took it.

"Okay, then."

The leather chair creaked as Morgan stood on the other side of the desk. "I guess we're finished."

"One more thing." Gabe stood up, too, and met his gaze.

"And that is?"

"My fiancée said you were at Happy Hearts the other day when she was there with Erica."

"That's right. My nephew loves going to see the animals."

"So it was a coincidence? You being there at the same time?"

Morgan sensed the other man's disapproval but he wasn't going to lie. "Actually, I ran into Erica in town. I mentioned that I'd be at the animal sanctuary with Robby."

Gabe nodded. "Mel said you and my sister were talking for a long time."

"Yeah." They'd laughed a lot, too. And Erica was the opposite of hard on the eyes. He'd enjoyed spending time with her more than anything he'd done in a long time. "She's easy to talk to."

"She's also pregnant, Dalton." There was a warning tone in his voice.

"And your point is?"

"She doesn't need someone like you complicating her life."

"Someone like me?" Morgan felt his temper flare but stopped short of telling this guy to go to hell. Mostly because he was Erica's brother. Why that should matter, he wasn't sure. But it did. He blew out a frustrated breath. "Not that I owe you an explanation, but we're friends."

"And that's all?"

"What more would I want?" Morgan's tone gave the man some of his warning back.

"You tell me." Gabe's eyes narrowed.

On some level Morgan was aware that this man was a big brother looking out for a younger sibling. He got that.

"I'm the oldest of five. I understand about keeping an eye on the younger ones. I only have brothers so I'm going to cut you some slack for being protective of your sister. I'm guessing that responsibility weighs a little heavier. So, I'll say this one more time. We're friends. Nothing more."

Gabe's look said he was going to hold Morgan to that. "Okay."

"I'll see myself out."

Morgan turned and headed out of the office, then back through the house to where he'd come in. He was frustrated and angry. How long would he have to live in Bronco Heights before he was good enough to be accepted by these people? It was a lesson, if he needed one, that money didn't buy everything. And then he saw Erica in the entryway by the front door and his irritation disappeared.

She looked fresh and pretty and made his heart skip and slide sideways in his chest. In her black leggings, long cream-colored sweater and cowboy boots, she looked beautiful. And when she saw him, she smiled with genuine warmth, which was just what he needed. Except that every time she smiled, he wondered how her lips would feel against his own.

"Morgan. What are you doing here?"

"I had some business with your brother."

She tipped her head to the side, studying him. "Did something happen?"

Other than Gabe declaring him off-limits to her? That still rubbed him the wrong way and irritated his sense of fairness. "Yes. I bought a herd bull from him."

"You don't look happy about it."

"No. It was a good deal," he said. Changing the subject, he asked, "What are you up to?"

"Just going for a walk. I've got to keep up my exercise. I used to ride horses but I can't now. It's a big no-no because of the risk of falling. That could harm the baby."

"Yeah. I can see that." He was oddly reluctant to say his goodbyes and leave. Glancing over his shoulder toward her brother's office, he frowned. Also, being warned off really bugged him, made him want to push back. "Would you like some company on your walk?"

"You don't need the exercise." She gave him a once-over and didn't seem to mind what she saw.

"A stroll with a pretty lady sounds like a healthy thing to do."

She flushed with pleasure at the compliment. "If you're sure, I wouldn't mind someone to talk to."

"Let's go." He took her jacket out of her hand and held it while she slid her arms into the sleeves. Then he opened the front door and let her precede him outside.

"Thanks."

"My pleasure." And that was the truth. She smelled really good. The scent of her hair and a certain fragrance that was uniquely her stirred in the air and burrowed inside him. *Nice* didn't even begin to describe what he was feeling. "Which way are we going?"

She pointed to a path that went behind the barn and corrals to a grass area and beyond. "Try and keep up."

"Someone's feeling pretty sassy today." He grinned.

"Yeah." Her smile faded as they headed out.

"Are you sure you're up for this? After all, you're walking for two."

"Funny. And I'm fine." She breathed deeply. "It's a beautiful day. The sun is out. It's all good."

"Okay."

They walked in silence for a while, surrounded by the sounds of nature. The birds singing, the whinny of a horse somewhere out of sight and a breeze that made tree leaves rustle.

"How's Robby?" she asked.

"Good. Rowdy. Healthy. Happy."

"Can't ask for more than that. Where's his mom? It seems like your brother was raising him alone before Amanda came into his life." She shrugged. "Women talk."

"His mother is in Colorado." But Morgan had a feeling that's not what she was asking. "She wasn't keen on being a mom. She sends presents for Christmas and birthdays but that's about it. Not hiding but not involved either."

"I see." With the toe of her boot she kicked a rock off the path and into the grass to the side. "He's a great kid."

"You'll get no argument from me about that."

"Can I ask you something?" she said hesitantly.

"Sure." But he braced himself.

"You're so good with Robby and clearly he loves you."

"I love him, too," Morgan said easily.

"But you don't want kids."

"Why do you say that?" he asked.

She looked up and the breeze blew a strand of hair across her face, into her eyes. She brushed it away and met his gaze. "The other day you seemed a little exasperated and said you don't know how your brother does it. That didn't sound like you were in favor of having the experience yourself."

"The truth is, I don't know if I'd be a very good father."

"I guess it would be hard to go for it if you have doubts." She slid her hands into the pockets of her jacket. "It was easy for me. There was no question in my mind about wanting to be a mom."

And she made it look good, he thought. But she was right. With his brother, the pregnancy happened and Holt manned up. He was all in when Robby was born, and Morgan would have done the same. But if he had a choice, it would be a tough call for him to make.

But that reminded him. "You had a doctor's appointment. How did that go?"

"Good."

Morgan hadn't known her long, but he felt as if he knew her well enough to see when something was bothering her. And that was now. He was certain of it.

"Did you like the doctor?"

"Yes. Very much." That might have been a little too enthusiastic. Compensating for something?

"Did someone give you a hard time? Was the office a dirty, windowless shack without running water and electricity?"

"It was fine."

He'd been going for the absurd to make her laugh. That was an epic fail and convinced him not to let up until she came clean about what was going on. "Tell me what's wrong, Erica. Please don't say *nothing*, because I can see different."

"Everything is good."

"I'm not buying that. Come on, this is me. Give it up." He met her gaze and saw in hers when she stopped pretending.

She left the dirt path and leaned against a tree. "I want to take a childbirth class. The doctor says it's not too late to do it."

"That's a good thing. No?"

"Yes and no." Her frown deepened. "I could use someone to go with me. A coach."

"Okay. So who's it going to be?" The baby's father? This wasn't the first time he'd wondered where the guy was. He was still curious, but it wasn't his place to push for information.

"That's just it. I don't know." She caught her top lip between her teeth.

"What about your mom?" he suggested.

She shook her head. "I can't ask her. As much as my parents nagged me about making them grandparents, their plan included marriage before motherhood. I need someone who is one hundred percent in my corner without making a judgment."

"You grew up here." From his perspective, that

was the family background someone needed to be accepted in Bronco Heights. "How about a friend?"

"I was gone so long I've lost touch with my friends. Or they've moved away." Her shoulders slumped and the sunshine in her face was all clouded over.

"What about Daphne Taylor?"

She shook her head. "We didn't stay in touch, and it seems presumptuous to ask. And Mel travels for her job. Even if that's only once or twice a month it could be inconvenient to rearrange her schedule, not to mention when I go into labor."

"There must be someone," he said.

"I don't know anyone I'd feel comfortable asking."

"You know me." Morgan couldn't hold back the words. Seeing her like this made him want to put the sparkle back in her eyes.

"You?" It wasn't quite a sparkle, but something jumped into her expression. "You do know this is a childbirth class?"

"Yeah."

"This inclination of yours to volunteer to help me out is getting to be a habit. It's very sweet, but I won't hold you to it."

Morgan wasn't sure why he felt so strongly about this. He was willing to admit that it was more than bonding over being outsiders. Mostly he just really liked her and couldn't help wanting to fix her problems.

"It's all right," he said. "You can hold me to it."

"Surely you're joking." She was incredulous.

"Nope. Dead serious."

"Why would you do it?"

"We're friends." And thrown into the mix was just a little bit of in-your-face to her brother for warning him off. "It's what friends do."

"But kids aren't your thing," she protested.

"You're doing the work. I'm being the support." He shrugged.

"But what if this baby is born in the middle of the night?" she challenged.

"It happens all the time with cows. I'm always on call."

"You didn't really just compare me to a cow," she teased. "Maybe I'm starting to look like one—"

"No way." He thought she was beautiful. "I didn't—I mean, I was just saying—"

"It's okay. I know what you meant. And I wouldn't ask you to be there for the labor—"

"What kind of friend would I be to abandon you? A coach doesn't train his players, then not show up for the game." Morgan shook his head.

"I'm completely blown away that you'd offer to do this for me. I just can't believe you would—"

"Well, believe it," he said firmly.

"I don't know what to say."

"For Pete's sake, just say yes and thank you."

"Okay. If you're absolutely sure… Yes." She laughed and looked as if a great weight was lifted from her shoulders. "I don't know why you would do this. And I'm not sure why it feels right, but it does. I'm very grateful to you. Thank you, Morgan."

When she looked at him the way she was now, as if he'd hung the moon, he would do anything for her. And it's not like this was forever. In a matter of weeks the baby would be here and his job would be done and their paths would take them in different directions. Probably he wouldn't see her and would miss that beautiful smile more than he wanted to admit.

A few days later Erica insisted on picking Morgan up for the birthing class. She knew where Dalton's Grange was and easily found his house on the property. She was early, which was a chronic thing with her because it had been drilled into her growing up that being late was rude. Now punctuality was a habit. As big as the baby was getting, she hoped this child would take after her and at least arrive on time.

Still, she wouldn't turn down the chance to check out his house. And she couldn't help being curious, especially when she noticed smoke curling out of the rock chimney and light pouring out of the windows making his home seem really warm and cozy and inviting.

She walked up to the wooden porch with the railing that spanned the front. The style was the same as the main house she'd passed, with a rock and log facade and peaked roof.

Her boots sounded on the porch as she walked up to the door and knocked. Moments later an older woman answered it. She had a blond bob hairdo, blue eyes and a welcoming smile.

"You must be Erica Abernathy. I'm Deborah, Morgan's mom."

Erica shook the hand she held out. "Nice to meet you."

It was. And it wasn't. Since he lived in his own house on the ranch, it hadn't occurred to her that she'd meet any of his relatives and have to explain her reason for being here. Especially when she hadn't told her own family about Morgan being her birthing coach.

"You are just the most adorable pregnant lady I've ever seen." The other woman beamed at her. It was the sort of look she'd hoped for from her own mother.

"I feel just the opposite of adorable," she said ruefully.

"Some women are lucky enough to barely look pregnant right up until giving birth. I have a feeling you're going to be like that." She shook her head. "This is the honest truth. I've had five babies and never looked as radiant as you."

"I'm not going to try and talk you out of that impression."

Deborah laughed. "Just to set the record straight,

no matter what it looks like, my son does not live with his mother."

"What a relief. That would be weird," she teased back.

"He was working on a project with his father and got back late, then had to feed and water the animals." She angled her head toward the hallway off the great room. "I brought him some dinner, which he wolfed down. He just went to shower and clean up."

Erica glanced around the room with a cheerful fire crackling in the hearth. Braided rugs were scattered over the wooden floor. A leather sofa and chairs were arranged on one big enough to accommodate the overstuffed furniture.

"I hope it's not a problem that I'm early." Another habit of hers was to prattle on and say too much when she was nervous. Like now. She made herself stop talking.

"Not at all. Morgan told me he's going to be your labor coach."

She felt the woman was only being chatty and nice, not fishing for gossip. To not give her a little information felt impolite. "Yes, he is. Your son is a kind, sympathetic and thoughtful man. It was the first thing I noticed about him when we met." Right after she'd rated him a solid fifteen on a one to ten hotness scale.

"He's always been that way. A sweet and sensitive little boy and a good man."

"I'll be a single mom, and I'm grateful he'll be my coach."

"He'll be a good one." The next obvious comment or question would be about the baby's father, but Deborah didn't bring it up.

Erica felt compelled to. "The baby's father isn't involved. Just so you know, there's no bad breakup or hard feelings in any way."

"Good to know." Deborah slid her hands into the pockets of her jeans.

This wasn't awkward at all. "Morgan tells me that you and your family have lived here for a year. How do you like it?"

"It's great." There was a little too much enthusiasm in her voice. "We came from a pretty small town in northern Montana. This is bigger. More civilization, I guess. Shopping, if you know what I mean."

"I do." She nodded, also with too much enthusiasm.

"My son said that you just returned to Bronco Heights."

"That's right. I went to college in Colorado and I ended up with a job there. But now I'm back home. My parents would be thrilled if I wasn't..." She looked down at her belly.

"Why do I get the feeling this homecoming wasn't

planned?" Deborah asked. Then she waved her hand and said, "Never mind. It was rude of me to ask."

"No, actually, I think you're psychic."

The woman laughed. "It's a mom thing. Gives a woman a sixth sense."

"Well, you're right. My company let me go. Coming home was plan B." Erica didn't want Morgan's mother to believe her a screwup, and gave her an abbreviated version of what happened. She wasn't exactly sure why she spilled her guts to this woman. The best thing she could come up with was that her son got his kindness and empathy genes from his mother. "In the end, my only option was to come back home."

"So your parents aren't thrilled about having their daughter back?"

"If they are, they're hiding it pretty well. They're old-fashioned."

"I'm sorry to hear that, Erica." She made an understanding sound.

"My family has expectations and I keep not meeting them."

"I'm sure they love you and just want what's best. For you to be happy."

"They absolutely do. I know that. And I want to make them proud, but I keep letting them down." Erica smiled sheepishly. "I'm sorry to dump all that on you. You're just easy to talk to."

"Your parents will come around, honey. Don't give up."

Just then Morgan walked into the room bringing with him the wonderful, masculine scents of soap and some spicy cologne. His hair was still damp from the shower and he was freshly shaved. In his plaid, snap-front shirt, jeans and boots he looked every inch the sexy cowboy he was. Erica felt that familiar flutter in her stomach, but this time her heartbeat kicked up, too.

"Sorry I'm running late," he said.

"No. I'm early." She hoped her voice wasn't as breathless as it sounded to her. And if it was, she prayed neither of the Daltons noticed. "Your mom and I have been talking. She assured me you aren't one of those men in his thirties who still lives with his mother. Although, she brings you food and that makes one wonder."

He simply grinned at the teasing. Erica got a little weak-kneed but chalked it up to simple appreciation for a good-looking man. Who was also being an exceptional friend.

"My mom is a good cook," he said. "It would be stupid to turn down a meal from her and she didn't raise any fools. It's one of her many talents. And it should be said that my brothers and I are all a little afraid of her."

Deborah laughed. "I always knew how to keep five unruly boys in line. Still do."

"I'd love to know your secret," Erica said.

She wasn't kidding. Obviously Morgan had a great relationship with his mother, and it was heart-warming to see. She wanted that with her child. It was also revealing to see him with the woman who'd raised him. She'd heard you could tell a lot about a man by the way he treated his mother. From what she could see, Morgan treated his mom with love and respect. He wasn't just a pretty face. He was a very good man.

"Please don't get her started on stories of the Dalton boys," he warned. "The naked baby pictures won't be far behind."

"I so want to make a pun out of what you just said." Erica laughed when he groaned.

"I think it's time for us to go. Now," he told her.

"Okay." She looked at his mom. "Can I drop you at the main house?"

"No, honey. I could use the walk. But thank you. I'll just gather up the dishes I brought." Deborah smiled and waved before walking into the kitchen.

Erica shivered when they went outside, and she told herself it was the chilly October evening not the nearness of Morgan. Inside her car, he was even closer, because he was tall and broad and built for a truck. Her heart did that bumping inside her chest thing again.

That made her hands shake a little and fumble as she inserted her key into the ignition. Eventually she managed and off they went, headed back the way she'd come. Past the main house with its log walls and big windows all lit up. Maybe the silence wasn't awkward, but it felt that way to her.

"Your mom is nice. Easy to talk to." Not nosy, Erica thought to herself. A good listener.

"Yeah, she's pretty great."

"I can't imagine raising five boys."

"Me either, but she made it look easy. She probably had the hang of it by the time my youngest brother came along."

"So, you told her about being my childbirth coach," Erica said casually.

"Yeah. When work ran late, she pitched in because I mentioned being late to the first class wasn't an option. Should I not have said anything?" There was a frown in his voice.

"No. Not at all. She was great about it. And didn't once share that you birth baby cows all the time."

He laughed. "Yeah. She's pretty cool about things. Always been there for me even when—"

His tone had turned sort of introspective, almost as if he'd forgotten she was there. Then he suddenly clammed up. There was a story, a personal one. Erica tried to be like his mom and not ask questions, but she was too darn curious.

"When what?" she prodded. "Something happened. Just so you know, I don't plan on letting this go. Friends talk to each other."

He was quiet for so long it appeared he wasn't going to answer. But finally he said, "I fell in love once. When I'd just turned twenty-one. I met a girl and felt the lightning strike."

That actually wasn't exactly what Erica had expected to hear. "Okay. And? There must be more."

"Unfortunately." He looked out the car window at the darkness going by. "I bought a ring, proposed, and she accepted. We set a date."

"But? I can hear one coming." She wished very much that there wasn't.

"About a week before the wedding I found out she was pregnant with another guy's baby. And she wasn't the one who told me."

"She was going to pass it off as yours?"

"She denied it, but I didn't believe her, what with not telling me and all." There was a trace of bitterness still in his voice.

That took her breath away. She shouldn't feel a parallel, because he wasn't in love with her, hadn't proposed, given her a ring or set a date. But, even though she hadn't slept with her baby's father, it surely was another man's child.

She managed to keep emotion out of her voice when she said, "So I guess you called off the wedding."

"Good guess." There was irony in his tone. "She made a fool out of me."

"Oh, Morgan, you were young and she was the

fool." To do that to a great guy like him was just really and truly stupid. "I gather from your tone that it put you off the whole notion of marriage."

"It's not high on my list," he agreed. "And that's not the only reason. My father is not anyone's example of the perfect husband."

"But your parents have overcome obstacles in their relationship and your mom seems happy. No regrets. She's given your dad a chance. Maybe you should, too."

"And maybe you should give your family a chance," he shot back.

Touché. She didn't say anything more but her mind was spinning. Such a personal and profound betrayal could explain why he was still not some lucky girl's husband and a father. That was a shame because he would be so good at both. As chances went, she would give him one in a heartbeat.

Chapter Six

Morgan hadn't planned to talk about his romantic crash and burn. A long time ago he put that unfortunate incident behind him, at least he thought he had. But suddenly the words were coming out of his mouth. One minute he was talking about how cool his mother was, and the next, he was confessing his past and explaining why marriage wasn't in his plans. All of this on the way to a childbirth class. What was wrong with this picture?

Too many things, but the only one that mattered was Erica. She was going through a tough time without a lot of support and he wouldn't turn his back on her, too.

"We're here." She turned the SUV into the parking lot of the Women's Health Center and found a space close to the entrance. "It's not too late to back out, Morgan. Speak now or forever hold your peace."

He opened the passenger door and the overhead light went on, illuminating the uncertainty in her expression. Every time he looked at her, all he could think about was fixing whatever problem she had. Tonight was no different.

"You can't get rid of me that easily," he assured her.

"Okay then." She retrieved a rolled up mat and pillow from the rear of the SUV. "Let's go learn something about birthing babies."

She smiled, and Morgan felt the power of it deep down inside. Fortunately there was no time to analyze his response because he had a feeling he wasn't going to like the results.

They made their way inside and up to a conference room at the far end of the top floor. When they walked in, the floor-to-ceiling windows revealed a beautiful view of Bronco, lights stretching to the base of the mountains.

The clock on the wall said five minutes to seven and not being late was a relief. Fixing fences had taken longer than anticipated today when he and his father had found more than one calf caught up. Freeing them without injury had taken time, and he didn't want to let Erica down, especially the first night of class. It was important to prove that she could count on him.

The rectangular room had a large open area at one end and three tables arranged in a U-shape with a lectern set up at the other. A woman in her late twenties stood there flipping through her notes. Three couples were already there, and Erica was looking around, eyes wide.

Morgan put his hand to the small of her back and fought the urge to pull her close. Only for reassurance. As a friend. "We should probably sit."

She glanced around one last time and nodded. "Right."

They found chairs at a right angle to a very young couple. The man smiled at him, the kind of look that implied sharing the ups, downs, joys and fears of this adventure, the one called fatherhood. The other two men nodded in his direction with similar expressions. Morgan noticed they were all wearing wedding rings, which made him the odd man out.

He didn't feel awkward or out of his element as much as he was relieved Erica wasn't facing this alone. But she wouldn't be if her baby's father was here. Up until now Morgan hadn't been all that curious, but this class highlighted the absence. What was the story?

That question would have to wait, because he had things to deal with now. The other people in this class probably thought he was going to be a father. There was no good reason he could think of to disabuse them of that impression. If it came up, he would let Erica take the lead. This was all about her.

The brunette standing behind the lectern glanced at the clock, then cleared her throat. "Everyone is here so let's get started. There's a lot of information to get through and you're on a deadline." There was chuckling and she waited a few moments before continuing. "My name is Carla McNicol. I'm a registered nurse and work in Labor and Delivery at the hospital. I'm also a certified childbirth educator. Why don't we start by quickly introducing ourselves."

The couple on the far side of the table started with first and last names, adding that this was their second baby. Married, as he'd suspected. The other two couples did the same. Then it was their turn.

"I'm Erica and this is Morgan. First baby," she said, "and I'm getting nervous."

"You've come to the right place," Carla assured her. "Knowledge is power. The more you know, the more in control you feel. This may be repetitious for second timers, but reminders never hurt. So, tonight I'm going to talk about things you can do to prevent preterm labor. You're all within weeks of delivery, but it's best for baby to stay put until nature takes its course."

She started with basics and Morgan was a little surprised at how very basic the things were. The importance of prenatal care. No alcohol or smoking. Prevent infections. Maybe use a condom during sex. He couldn't resist looking at Erica, and her cheeks were bright pink. The RN got as basic as taking care of teeth, keeping gums healthy. Although Carla teased that she was sure couples conscientious enough to take this class already brushed and flossed.

"Believe it or not, stress and avoiding it as much as possible is a very big factor in preventing labor too early," she pointed out. "If there's job tension, do what you can to minimize it. People who make your blood pressure spike—and we all have them in our lives—politely but firmly distance yourself as much as possible. Grandparents mean well but they can add to your tension. Do what you need to do to put yourselves first, Moms."

Carla talked about family-centered maternity care in the hospital, methods for pain management and birth options. She said there would be more information on that presented in upcoming classes.

"And the last thing we're going to do is go over relaxation techniques. I'll demonstrate tonight, but I can't emphasize this enough. Practice makes perfect. The goal is to relax your entire body while one muscle contracts. Your uterus needs to push down and retract the cervix. If other muscles are tight during contractions, you're wasting energy and oxygen. This technique also helps with stress."

She directed them to spread their mats on the

floor. Erica sat with her legs crisscrossed, knees out, while Morgan knelt behind her. Carla demonstrated deep breaths to fill the lungs, then exhaling while concentrating on relaxing other parts of the body. Doing it daily would help moms-to-be master conditioned responses to a labor coach's commands.

"I recommend practicing these techniques every night in bed," Carla said. "And that's it for tonight. I look forward to seeing everyone next week."

Erica was thoughtful and quiet as they rolled up the mat, collected the pillow and were the first ones to walk outside to the parking lot. No chatting after class. No awkward questions to be answered. He could feel her tension and remembered what the RN had said about avoiding it. She hit a button on her key fob and the rear hatch of the SUV slowly lifted.

Morgan put the mat and pillow in the car, then held out his hand. "Give me the keys."

"What?"

"Your keys," he said again.

"Why? Is this a carjacking?"

"If I was going to rip off a pregnant lady, she'd need to be driving one heck of a fine truck." They were standing under a light and he met her gaze, bracing for her stubborn streak to kick in and push back. "I'm driving. Take some stress off you."

She hesitated a moment, then nodded and set the keys in his open palm. "Okay."

Obviously she was lost in her own thoughts, because there was no conversation until he pulled the SUV into the parking lot of The Daily Grind, a coffee shop at the edge of town.

"Why are we stopping here?" she asked.

"I just thought before going home you might need to talk."

"Why would you think that?" She didn't deny it.

"Because you're not talking at all, and it's kind of freaking me out."

She sighed. "Coffee is a nice idea but I've already had my ration of caffeine for the day."

"I think this place has tea, without the kicker. Or water. Until tonight I had no idea you were supposed to drink that much." He looked over at her. "And I bet you wouldn't say no to dessert. Coach is buying."

She shook her head. "I should treat you. I had no idea—"

He put a finger to her lips to stop her words. The jolt he got from touching her nearly stopped his heart. "Arguing is stressful. My treat. End of discussion."

"Okay."

At the counter she ordered a caffeine-free herbal tea and a pumpkin scone. He got black coffee and paid for everything. They carried their stuff to a table in a far corner and sat.

He blew on his steaming cup. "So, what's on your mind?"

"I wouldn't hold it against you if you want to back

out." Her tone said that's what she expected. "I had no idea this class would be so…" She didn't finish the thought, but added, "If this experience is too weird for you, I completely understand."

"If you're okay, I'm okay."

"I am more than okay," she said. "I was very glad you were there. As long as you're sure—"

"Yes, I'm sure. We're friends. I feel as if I've known you for years." But he saw that she was still anxious. "What else is bothering you?"

She looked up, her hazel eyes more brown than green and very uneasy. "This class made it all real. There's only one way out of this. I don't know if I can do it."

"You can."

"Just like that?" she asked.

"Yeah. And there's the fact that there's no way out except birth." He shrugged. "We'll practice the breathing, go to the classes and you'll feel prepared."

"I desperately want to believe you so I'm going to." She smiled at him. "Thank you."

"Anytime."

But he was standing in for another man. That made him curious and a little bothered by the lack of information about her baby's father. The guy had to be a jerk to not be around for her.

Was she still in love with him? Morgan hoped not and the intensity of that feeling surprised—and worried—him.

* * *

When Morgan stopped at his house, Erica thanked him again for going with her, then headed home to the Ambling A. All the way she kept seeing the questions in his eyes. In class tonight he'd looked perfectly comfortable with all the information, even when she'd blushed to the roots of her hair at the mention of condoms during sex.

But when they stopped for coffee, after he'd reassured her he was her friend and would help her get through this, his expression grew more thoughtful. She knew he was wondering why he was there instead of the baby's father. Should she tell him?

That rolled around in her mind as she parked her car near the main house. No one had been around earlier when she went to pick up Morgan, so she'd left a note. The front porch light was on but she hoped no one was waiting up for her. Partly because her parents had to get up early to do ranch work. And partly because she knew there would be questions about where she'd been. Talking about anything to do with the baby seemed to create more tension.

Carefully opening the front door, she slipped inside as quietly as possible, then turned to close it. When footsteps sounded behind her, she knew stealth had been futile.

She whirled around. "Mama. I thought you'd be in bed."

"Your father is. I was watching TV in the other room. Waiting up for you."

"I'm sorry." It was sweet but sort of made her feel like a teenager sneaking in after curfew. "You didn't have to do that."

"I know." Angela stifled a yawn and pulled her long sweater more snugly around her. "But it's a funny thing. When you lived in Denver, I didn't actively worry about you coming in at night. Now that you're here, I can't relax until I know you're home safe and sound."

"But I'm a grown woman," she protested.

"Doesn't matter. You'll always be my baby." Her gaze dropped to Erica's pregnant belly. "You'll understand one of these days."

"I didn't mean to keep you up."

"It's okay." Her mom smiled. "Are you hungry? How about a cup of tea to warm you up? It's chilly outside."

"I'd love one." This was nice. It reminded Erica of the closeness they'd shared before she'd gone away to college.

They walked into the kitchen together, and her mom filled a teakettle with water and put it on the stove, lighting the burner beneath it. Erica pulled two mugs out of the cupboard and found her mom's stash of tea bags. Her father and Gabe had no use for anything but coffee, so this ritual was something only she and her mother shared.

Erica chose something decaffeinated that promised peaceful rest. She showed her mother and laughed. "I won't hold my breath about that since I'll probably be up peeing half the night."

"That's my nightly go-to tea." Her mom grinned. "But I'll be racing you to the bathroom."

Erica laughed. "It's like old times."

"I've missed this." Angela's expression was wistful. "You used to come home at night and tell me about what happened with you and your friends. Your dates. I remember the first time you went out with Jordan Taylor."

"Yeah. I was pretty stoked that a former high school big man on campus and local legend like him would even notice me, let alone ask me on a date."

"Do you think you gave him a fair shot?" her mom wondered.

"Mama, we've been over this." A few dates with the son of the wealthiest rancher in town had been part of the parental push to get her to stay home and attend a local college. "He was like a brother. There was no chemistry at all, no lightning strike."

Not like with Morgan Dalton, she thought. They had declared themselves friends tonight, but her strong feelings for him didn't fit neatly into that box. Under different circumstances she would be hoping for more, but with the baby coming, a friendship was all they'd ever have.

"Too bad." The kettle whistled and her mom filled

the two mugs. They carried them over to the table and sat, just like in the old days.

Angela blew on the steamy tea. "Your note only said that you were going out. Where were you tonight?"

Suddenly the warm, fuzzy, nostalgic feeling was replaced by wariness. Being able to go home again was an illusion. You could physically be there but emotionally it would never be the same.

The walls went up. "Oh, nowhere special."

Her mother's eyes said she didn't miss the evasive tactic. "What did you do?"

"Oh, you know—" Erica wasn't prepared to talk about this. She wanted mother-daughter warm and fuzzy, not tension and judgment.

"Actually I don't know. That's why I'm asking." Her tone hinted at hurt feelings. "Did it have something to do with Morgan Dalton?"

"Why would you ask that?"

"Gabe said he was here recently on ranch business and then you took a long walk with him." She dunked her tea bag with more force than seemed necessary. "And Mel said he offered to take you to the Denim and Diamonds fundraiser next month."

"That's true."

"Which part?" Her mother frowned. "The walk or the asking out?"

"Both, actually." Erica was not going to say more

but decided to add one last thing. "I like him. He's a good man."

"You haven't known him very long."

"Sometimes you don't have to know someone a long time. You can just tell."

"You were with him tonight, weren't you?"

She had to give the woman something. "I was at a childbirth class tonight."

"Oh." That seemed to appease her mother. "How was it?"

"Interesting. I'm a little nervous about the birth." This woman had been through it twice in addition to emotionally painful miscarriages. She knew how it felt. "Does it hurt, Mama?"

Angela's expression turned soft, a combination of sympathy and concern. "I want badly to lie and tell you it doesn't. But I can't. Yes, honey, it does hurt. But it's nothing you can't handle. And when you see your baby… There's just no feeling in the world like it. It's worth everything you go through."

That's what Morgan had said. The part where she could handle it. That helped some. "I'm still a little nervous."

"That's completely normal. Trust me, by the time this baby comes you'll be so ready to do whatever it takes to bring him or her into the world. The childbirth class will help with those nerves—" She stopped and her bonding-mom expression was replaced by something more skeptical. "I thought you needed someone to go to those classes with you. A coach."

"It's recommended." *Please don't ask more*, she silently begged.

"Do you have one?"

She hesitated and thought about a lie, but this was her *mother*. And dishonesty never ended well. "Yes, I do."

"Who?"

Erica sighed. "Morgan."

Surprise and disappointment battled for dominance in her mother's eyes. There was no sympathy or concern now. Just more hurt feelings. "Why him?"

"You and Dad and Gabe have made your negative opinion clear. I didn't feel I could ask you. Mel is a sweetheart, but I don't want to compromise her relationship with my brother. I don't know anyone else. Morgan has been there for me since I came home. There was no judgment." She shrugged. "And he offered."

"Oh, Erica—" She shook her head. Her mother sighed. "I'm concerned about you and how difficult it will be for you being a single mother."

"I gave it a lot of thought, believe me. But more than anything I want to be a mother. If I have to do it alone, then so be it. If I'd had anywhere else to go, I would have. As soon as I find a job I'll move out."

"Erica, no one is asking you to leave."

"I know. But I think it would be better if I did."

"You are more than welcome to stay. This is your home, and we love having you here. But I completely support your decision, whatever that is." Her mother stared at her, eyes suspiciously bright. She stood, leaving her now-cold tea untouched. "I'm going up to bed. Sleep well, sweetie."

"Good night, Mama." She watched the woman she loved so much walk away.

Just then the back door opened and Malone walked in. This man with the craggy face and bushy mustache was no one's idea of what a cook looked like. And he was the walking, talking explanation of why it wasn't wise to judge a book by its cover. He had a way with food. And not just meat and potatoes. His sauces were to die for and he made biscuits from scratch that melted in your mouth.

"Hi, Malone." She settled her elbow on the table and rested her cheek in her palm.

"Hey, Erica. Missed you at dinner tonight." It was dark outside, but the man still wore his tattered old hat and a bandanna tied around his neck. But the look worked with his old jeans, boots and faded plaid cotton shirt. "There's leftover chicken if you're hungry."

"I'm not." A pumpkin scone had taken care of that. "Why are you here?"

"Gonna get a head start on breakfast. Omelets tomorrow. If everything is cut up and ready I can whip them up in a jiffy." He angled his head toward her obvious condition. "If there's anything you're craving, just let me know."

"I will."

"Once knew a pregnant lady who had to have her avocados." He grinned. "And melons—cantaloupe, honeydew, watermelon—didn't matter which."

"Right now I can't say I have any cravings." At least nothing that food would fix.

"You feelin' all right? That baby giving you trouble?"

Yes, but not the way he meant. "No, I'm fine."

"Don't look like it," he observed.

"There's still some tension between Mama and I."

He sat his six-foot frame into the chair her mother had recently vacated. This man was a talker and he was settling in. "It was awful hard on your mama and daddy when you went away."

"I know. But it's my life. Shouldn't I be able to live it my way?"

"Yup. And they know that." His eyes were piercing. "It may not be my place to say but look at the view from their front porch. You come home without telling them there's gonna be a baby. Now here you are, and that little one is going to be here real soon. And their feelings were hurt. They might just need a minute or two to adjust."

She sighed. As much as she wanted to argue with him, she couldn't. When she lived here Malone had more than once put in his two cents and she'd missed his plain-spoken wisdom. "You're right. I should have said something right away. I just couldn't face what I knew I'd hear in their voices and see in their eyes. I only ever want them to be proud of me."

"They are, honey. But what with you working and living somewhere else, they didn't get much chance to fiddle with their feelings about you being all grown-up. It's hard for parents to figure out how not to butt in and try to keep their kids from making mistakes."

"This baby isn't a mistake. I've wanted to be a mother for a long time now."

He smiled and patted her hand. "And you'll be a good one, too. Just like your mama."

"Thanks, Malone." She smiled sadly. "For just a little while tonight Mama and I were having such a nice talk. Just like we used to. Then it went bad. They say you can't go home again, and I probably shouldn't have."

"Well, you did, though. And things have changed. My advice is remember the old while you're making the now new. And it doesn't happen overnight."

"That sounds like good advice."

"It is. But worth what you paid for it." He grinned, then stood up. "Gotta get going on my chores. Breakfast comes awful early around here."

"Can I give you a hand?"

"That's okay, honey. You should get some rest. The baby needs it."

She stood, too, then went up on tiptoe to kiss his cheek. "Thanks for the talk. I'll do my best to make the now new."

And until this baby was born, the new included Morgan. He was a new she could easily get used to.

Chapter Seven

Along with lawyer and doctor appointments and birthing class, Erica was busy sending out résumés. She was encouraged by quick responses to them asking for interviews. But after the second one without an offer of employment, she was forced to admit two things. Because she'd been hired at Barron Enterprises as a college intern, she didn't realize what a challenge job hunting could be. The second thing was that being very pregnant didn't make the search any easier.

This was her third interview, one she'd actually scheduled before moving back. She was sitting across the desk from Sandra Allen, the Human Resources director of an energy company in downtown Bronco Heights. This was a face-to-face meeting for their accounting/marketing position, following a phone interview during which this same woman had seemed very enthusiastic. Probably Erica should have mentioned being pregnant, but she just wanted a foot in the door, an opportunity to display her personality and business knowledge. One look at Erica's well-developed baby bump had cooled off any interest.

She knew what the woman was thinking because she'd had to deal with personnel issues like this at her last job. She needed to get ahead of it, so to speak, then highlight the skills she could bring to the table in the long term.

She smiled. "You probably noticed that I'm pregnant. My due date is next month and I already have child care arranged." That was a lie but she would make it true. "If you decide to hire me, I'll get to know the company, and when I return from maternity leave, I can hit the ground running." She was going to throw everything at the wall and hope something stuck. "In my previous job, I was in charge of day-to-day operations. I oversaw Human Resources, accounting, marketing and IT."

Sandra folded her hands and rested them on her desk. "You have an impressive résumé, Erica."

"Thank you." She was pretty sure she heard a "but" in the woman's voice but hoped she was wrong.

"The thing is," she continued, "you're overqualified for the job we have. Upper management would be a better fit and we just don't have an opening right now."

"You're concerned that I'll leave if something better comes along." It was about more than that, but she was determined to leave it all on the table. "As you can see from my work history, I was hired during my college internship and stayed with the company for eight years. That shows a high degree of loyalty. If you give me a chance, I won't let you down."

"I have no doubt." The woman nodded. "But you should know that I have more people to interview. So, when that process is complete, I'll make a decision. I will call you one way or the other. Thanks for coming in."

Erica knew that was a "don't let the door hit you in the backside on the way out." She stood and shook the other woman's hand. "I appreciate your time."

She walked out of the office and left the building. It was hard not to be discouraged, even though she understood why hiring someone in her condition was a risk. On top of being discouraged, she was starving. And needing someone to listen to her bitch and moan. She knew just the place where both needs could be met and a short time later she walked into DJ's Deluxe looking for Mel. The restaurant's new manager directed her to a large office upstairs.

She found it and stood in the doorway, taking in the cushy conversation area and large desk with a computer. Mel sat behind it and was so engrossed, she didn't even know she had a visitor.

"Knock, knock."

Mel looked up and it took two beats for her to register recognition. "Hey. Sorry. I was so focused. What are you doing here?"

"I'm hungry. And I need a friendly face and sympathetic ear."

"Well, you've come to the right place. Am I wrong that you want privacy for this conversation?"

"You are not wrong."

The other woman stood and walked around her desk. "I'll get you some food. Anything you're craving? Cheesecake? Death by chocolate?"

"Call me a peasant, but a burger and fries would be just about the best thing ever," Erica said.

"Coming right up." She indicated one of the chairs in front of her desk. "Have a seat."

"Thanks."

Erica sat and closed her eyes for a moment, breathing in and out. Trying to relax the way Carla, the childbirth educator, had instructed. This scenario was not what she planned for her baby and the least she could do was try to neutralize her stress. She knew her family wouldn't put her and the baby on the street, but the judgment would always be in their eyes.

The one unexpected positive was Morgan. Literally without any questions asked, he was there for her and the baby. He calmed her when they were to-gether. And she was happy around him. He was a friendly port in a storm of tension and hormones. A bright spot in an otherwise challenging chapter of her life. Once upon a time she'd naively believed she could pull off perfect for this baby, but now she knew better. The best she could do would have to be good enough and at least she had Morgan.

It wasn't long before Mel returned with a plate. She set it on the edge of the desk. "Dig in and feed that baby."

"You don't have to tell me twice."

Erica ate a couple of the fries and closed her eyes in ecstasy. "Best thing I have ever tasted."

"That happens when you're starving. Although DJ's Deluxe sets a high bar in all its restaurants."

"I only care about this one. Right here, right now." She cut the burger in half to make it manageable.

For a few moments there was only silence in the room, if one excluded her appreciative moans. After the first half was gone, she took a break and sat back in her chair.

Erica looked at the lovely woman who was going to marry her brother. "You're a lifesaver. Almost lit-erally. I thank you, and my unborn baby, your future nephew or niece, thanks you."

"Don't mention it. Happy to help." She was sit-ting behind the desk again, frowning at all the pa-perwork in front of her. "With great power comes great responsibility. I'm grateful to you for giving me an excuse to take a break."

"It's the least I can do for family."

"That means a lot." Mel's smile was sweet and soft. "You know, before you came back home, I was a little nervous about meeting Gabe's sister."

"Me? Why?" She wiped her hands on her napkin and crumpled it in her hand.

"You're important to him. And he's important to me. I'm an only child and I lost my parents six years ago. So, I feel as if I'm not just getting the best guy in the world, but a family, too."

"Aww..." Erica felt an emotional lump in her throat. That happened a lot lately.

"You and I have hit it off even better than I'd hoped. I've never had a sister and always wanted one."

"Me, too." She reached a hand across the desk and Mel took it, squeezed affectionately. "You're going to make me cry."

"I would take that as a compliment, except I'm guessing pregnancy hormones might make you emotional if I said *the sky is blue*."

Erica laughed. "You're not completely wrong."

"Speaking of family..." Mel folded her hands and put them on top of her desk. "Have you seen Josiah since you've been home?"

Erica knew the other woman wasn't trying to make her feel guilty, but she did anyway. Gabe had told her Gramps was in Snowy Mountain, a facility north of Bronco Heights that offered a full range of services, from independent living to caring for patients with dementia or Alzheimer's. "Not yet. I've had a lot to deal with since I got home, and it hasn't been that long. I had to see a lawyer. And had a doctor's appointment. A couple of job interviews."

"I understand," Mel said. Clearly she meant that. "It's just that I'm so frustrated. We've hit a wall finding his daughter Beatrix and aren't sure what to do next. More than anything I'd like to give Winona some peace about her child, the comfort of knowing she's all right. Josiah has occasional lucid moments. Gabe and I are wondering if seeing you might just jolt him out of wherever he is and get him to give us something."

Erica sighed. "I feel so bad that I haven't visited yet."

"I know. But try to see him soon if you can." Mel nodded sympathetically. "And I'll stop now. How's the job search going?"

"Not so good."

"Is that what you wanted to talk about?" the other woman asked.

"Yes." Now it was Erica's turn to be frustrated. "I understand what's going through their mind when they look at me so pregnant. I used to deal with this situation, but on the other side of the desk, so to speak. If hired, I would work my butt off for just a few weeks, then have a baby and leave them short-handed again. I could be back to work in six weeks, if all goes as planned. But what if it doesn't? If I was making the decision and had two equal candidates for one position, but one was very pregnant, the best business decision would be to hire the other one."

"I hear you." Mel sighed. "For women, work and motherhood is always going to be a balancing act."

"That's the best you've got?" Erica was only half kidding.

"Yeah. So let's talk about something more pleasant."

"I'm open to suggestions."

"You've met Amanda, but not our friend Brittany yet. She's the one organizing the Denim and Diamonds fundraiser. Apparently it's all coming together really well."

"Great."

"Are you planning to go? If the baby hasn't come yet? I know you said Jordan Taylor's father isn't your favorite person."

"True. But I wouldn't mind seeing Jordan. He and I managed to stay friends even after dating a short time."

Mel nodded. "I can see why your folks got their hopes up. His father and uncles own Taylor Beef. Not only is he good-looking, he'll never have to worry about money."

"I should hope not. It's a big company." And sud-

"4 for 4" MINI-SURVEY

We are prepared to **REWARD** you with 4 FREE Books and Free Gifts for completing our MINI SURVEY!

Romance

Wholesome Romance

You'll get up to...

4 FREE BOOKS & FREE GIFTS

FREE
Value Over
$20!

just for participating in our Mini Survey!

Get Up To 4 Free Books!

Dear Reader,

IT'S A FACT: if you answer 4 quick questions, we'll send you 4 FREE REWARDS from each series you try!

Try **Harlequin® Special Edition** books featuring comfort and strength in the support of loved ones and enjoying the journey no matter what life throws your way.

Try **Harlequin® Heartwarming™ Larger-Print** books featuring uplifting stories where the bonds of friendship, family and community unite.

Or **TRY BOTH!**

I'm not kidding you. As a leading publisher of women's fiction, we value your opinions... and your time. That's why we are prepared to reward you handsomely for completing our mini-survey. In fact, we have 4 Free Rewards for you, including 2 free books and 2 free gifts from each series you try!

Thank you for participating in our survey,

Pam Powers

To get your 4 FREE REWARDS:
Complete the survey below and return the insert today to receive up to 4 FREE BOOKS and FREE GIFTS guaranteed!

"4 for 4" MINI-SURVEY

1 Is reading one of your favorite hobbies?

☐ YES   ☐ NO

2 Do you prefer to read instead of watch TV?

☐ YES   ☐ NO

3 Do you read newspapers and magazines?

☐ YES   ☐ NO

4 Do you enjoy trying new book series with FREE BOOKS?

☐ YES   ☐ NO

Please send me my Free Rewards, consisting of **2 Free Books from each series I select** and **Free Mystery Gifts**. I understand that I am under no obligation to buy anything, as explained on the back of this card.

❏ Harlequin® Special Edition (235/335 HDL GQ4M)
❏ Harlequin® Heartwarming™ Larger Print (161/361 HDL GQ4M)
❏ Try Both (235/335 & 161/361 HDL GQ4X)

FIRST NAME	LAST NAME

ADDRESS

APT.#	CITY

STATE/PROV.	ZIP/POSTAL CODE

EMAIL ❏ Please check this box if you would like to receive newsletters and promotional emails from Harlequin Enterprises ULC and its affiliates. You can unsubscribe anytime.

SE/HW-820-MS20

HARLEQUIN READER SERVICE—Here's how it works:

Accepting your 2 free books and 2 free gifts (gifts valued at approximately $10.00 retail) places you under no obligation to buy anything. You may keep the books and gifts and return the shipping statement marked "cancel." If you do not cancel, approximately one month later we'll send you more books from the series you have chosen, and bill you at our low, subscribers-only discount price. Harlequin® Special Edition books consist of 6 books per month and cost $4.99 each in the U.S or $5.74 each in Canada, a savings of at least 17% off the cover price. Harlequin® Heartwarming™ Larger-Print books consist of 4 books per month and cost just $5.74 each in the U.S. or $6.24 each in Canada, a savings of at least 21% off the cover price. It's quite a bargain! Shipping and handling is just 50¢ per book in the U.S. and $1.25 per book in Canada*. You may return any shipment at our expense and cancel at any time — or you may continue to receive monthly shipments at our low, subscribers-only discount price plus shipping and handling. *Terms and prices subject to change without notice. Prices do not include sales taxes which will be charged (if applicable) based on your state or country of residence. Canadian residents will be charged applicable taxes. Offer not valid in Quebec. Books received may not be as shown. All orders subject to approval. Credit or debit balances in a customer's account(s) may be offset by any other outstanding balance owed by or to the customer. Please allow 3 to 4 weeks for delivery. Offer available while quantities last.

▲ If offer card is missing write to: Harlequin Reader Service, P.O. Box 1341, Buffalo, NY 14240-8531 or visit www.ReaderService.com ▲

BUSINESS REPLY MAIL
FIRST-CLASS MAIL   PERMIT NO. 717   BUFFALO, NY

POSTAGE WILL BE PAID BY ADDRESSEE

HARLEQUIN READER SERVICE
PO BOX 1341
BUFFALO NY 14240-8571

NO POSTAGE
NECESSARY
IF MAILED
IN THE
UNITED STATES

denly flashes went off in her brain. There might be a job opening for her in that big company.

"And his father is putting on this big charity shin-dig to raise money for programs to help lower income families in Bronco Valley. I'm going to need a shin-dig kind of dress," Mel said.

Erica looked ruefully at her belly. "I'm going to need a tent."

"Oh please. You hardly look pregnant and you're beautiful." Mel toyed with a pen. "At least Morgan thinks so."

"How do you know?"

"I saw the way he looked at you that day at the animal sanctuary."

"You're imagining things."

"Am I? Because right after I noticed that, he asked you for a date."

"No. It's more like he offered to be my body-guard."

Mel looked skeptical. "How do you explain him volunteering to be your labor coach?"

"Mom told you."

"Yeah." The other woman looked concerned. "And it makes one wonder why."

"Because he's a really nice guy."

"Your family is nice, too."

"I couldn't agree more. But they don't approve of my decision to have this baby alone. I couldn't ask my father. Which would be really weird anyway. My mother is concerned about me being a single mom so I guess I'm trying to prove I can handle the challenges that come up. And you're engaged to Gabe, who thinks I've lost my mind. So I didn't want you in the middle of it," she explained. "Morgan is my good friend. I don't feel like I fit in here anymore, and he feels as if he hasn't been welcomed into the community with open arms." She shrugged. "We get each other."

"Okay."

Erica could see the other woman still had something on her mind. "Go ahead. Sisters can tell each other things that no one else could get away with. Spit it out."

"It's just…" Mel sighed. "Things between you and Morgan seem to be moving pretty fast. I'm afraid you're vulnerable and you'll get hurt."

"He wouldn't hurt me. You'd think a man that good-looking would be a jerk, but he's not. I met his mom and can see why." She thought for a moment. "And your friend Amanda is engaged to his brother. Do you approve of him?"

"Well, yes, but—"

"No buts." Erica held up her hands. "Morgan won't hurt me. It's not like that between us. He doesn't want me that way. I'm pregnant. In fact, no one wants me."

"That's not true."

"Feels true."

After Peter, she'd given up on dating, but being with Morgan gave her a glimpse of possibilities and she had to remember that none of the possibilities included forever with him. She was almost sorry that all of it would change when the baby was born and she wouldn't have a reason to see him anymore.

When Morgan pulled his truck to a stop in front of the main house on the Ambling A, the front door opened immediately and Erica walked out. She must have been waiting for him. That could only mean tension with her family, quite possibly because of him, and she was trying to head it off. He was all in favor of steering clear of stress for her and the baby, but facing the Abernathys didn't bother him.

He'd been surprised but really stoked when she called and suggested going to the Bronco Harvest Festival, so here he was to pick her up. He got out of the truck and went around to the passenger door to open it for her.

"Hi," he said.

She smiled up at him. "You're very punctual."

"So are you." He watched her put a foot on the running board, then handed her into the truck. When she was settled in the seat, her face was very close to his. Her breath was soft on his cheek and her slightly parted lips were a whisper away.

Leaning in to see if they were as soft and sweet as he imagined would be so easy, and he really wanted to. It wasn't the first time the thought crossed his mind. But—no.

He met her gaze. "I would have come up to the door, like the gentleman my mother taught me to be."

"I was ready and waiting. Wanted to save you the trouble."

It was late in the afternoon, and the sun was setting behind the big house, putting them in shadow. Still, Morgan was almost sure her cheeks turned pink and her voice was a little too perky, even by Erica standards. "You didn't want me to come inside, say hi to the family."

She stared at him for a couple of beats, then sighed. "I'm protecting you. They've got some stupid idea that you're pretending to be interested in me because you want to take advantage of me somehow."

That burned because it was so off the mark. But showing anger wouldn't help, so he deflected with a smart-ass comment. "They're right."

"Really?"

"Yes. I'm using you. Before you, I was just a misfit outsider. Now I'm a misfit outsider who's taking the prettiest lady in Bronco Heights to the Harvest Festival."

"I'm taking you to the Harvest Festival, remember?" Her wariness slipped away and she grinned. "You, sir, are a sweet talker."

"And don't you forget it."

"Well, I'm using you right back. It's way past time

my family gets the message that I'm a grown woman. Strong and independent. They can't tell me who I can or cannot see socially." She caught herself and added, "Or who my friends are."

"So I'm your rebellion guy?" He couldn't help smiling.

"I know I'm a little old for that, but now that I'm back, ground rules need to be set," she said firmly.

"Hey, I'm just glad you called."

"It's not much," she said, "but I really want to thank you. I'm very grateful not to be the only woman in that birthing class without a coach."

"Happy to help." He closed the door and went around to the driver's side, then got in. "So, how are you?" he asked as he drove away.

"Still unemployed and guilt ridden."

"You might want to give me some context for that statement."

"Yeah." She sighed. "I had three interviews and got zero job offers. They take one look at me and it's game over."

"I'm sorry to hear that." And he wanted badly to fix her situation but kept that to himself. "And the guilt?"

"Mel reminded me I haven't been to see Gramps yet. It's no excuse, but I've had a lot to do since I moved back."

"That's the truth."

"Mel thinks seeing me might shake him up, provoke a lucid moment so he'll give up something that will help us find his daughter."

Morgan shook his head. "I can't imagine having a child and not knowing where they are, or anything about them."

"That child would be in her seventies now," Erica said. "Mel wants to find her and bring her to her mother so that Winona can see her daughter and know she's all right. But Mel is getting discouraged about finding a lead."

He happened to glance over and saw her put her hands protectively on her belly. Erica was already shielding her child. No way she'd give it up, and he deeply respected her commitment.

"I'd sure like to help find her," he said. "If there's anything I can do, let me know."

"Thanks, Morgan. I wish there was. But aren't you getting tired of doing me favors?" she teased.

"No." It'd be another reason to be with Erica, and he relished that. In fact, it was getting harder to think the time would come when she wasn't in his life anymore.

A short time later they arrived at the Bronco Fairgrounds. Local law enforcement was directing traffic, and Morgan followed the line of cars to an unpaved field where vehicles lined up in rows.

He parked the truck and looked over at her. "You ready to do this?"

"Yes. I haven't been to one of these since before I went away to college. I used to love it."

The sun had gone down, but large spotlights were strategically placed around the big, open field. The parking area was on a rise, and as they walked toward the festival entrance, the expanse of activities was spread out before them. There were carnival rides, booths with games and a bouncy house for the kids. Strings of white lights were hung around the whole area.

"This is bigger than I remember," she said, eyes wide.

"It's my first time, so I have nothing to compare it to."

Just inside the entrance there was a temporary enclosure holding animals. Daphne Taylor was in the middle of it surrounded by a sheep, a baby goat, a pony and the pig—Tiny Tim. She was supervising children as they petted the docile creatures. In the line of kids awaiting their turn, he recognized his brother, Holt, with Amanda and Robby.

"Hey, you guys." Morgan squatted down to eye level with his nephew. "Hi, dude. Haven't you had enough of the animals yet?"

"No." The little guy vigorously shook his head. "There are dogs and cats here, too. For adoption." His blue eyes were big, bright and eager.

Erica said hello and looked up at his brother. "We haven't met. I'm Erica Abernathy."

"Nice to meet you." If Holt was surprised about the pregnancy or the fact that Morgan was with her, it didn't show.

"Daddy, I want to adopt another dog," Robby said. "They need a good home. It says so on the sign."

"Whoa, kid." His father held up his hands. "We're here to pet the animals. That's all. Remember?"

"Yes." But the boy pointed to the separate enclosure, where several pudgy puppies were running around and tumbling over each other. "There's a black-and-white one over there, and he keeps lookin' at me."

Erica laughed. "You're in trouble now, Dad. If you can figure out how to say no to that eager little face, I'd appreciate you sharing the secret."

"Start practicing now." Holt grinned. "So, what are you two going to do?"

"Not sure yet." Morgan looked down at her. "We just got here. I figured we'd just browse and then see what grabs us." And then he couldn't resist saying, "Hey, Robby, that black-and-white pup is really cute. I think he's smiling at you again."

Holt gave him a look that could laser paint off the barn. "There will be retaliation. You won't know when or where, but it will happen."

Morgan laughed. "Bring it, brother. See you later, guys."

He put his hand to Erica's back, guiding her through the crowd. But with all the people moving every which way, they kept getting separated. So he took her hand in his. "I don't want to lose you."

"And I don't want to be lost." She squeezed his fingers and smiled up at him.

They meandered up and down the rows of booths containing food and games. She stopped by a giant ring toss game and admired the stuffed bears it had for prizes.

"Let's win one for the baby," he said.

She eyed him skeptically. "It might be less expensive to just buy one at the store."

"You doubt my skill?"

"I didn't say that."

"Not in so many words." He walked over to the woman taking money and bought five rings. Three out of five would win a prize. "I never back down from a challenge."

"You could light that money on fire and have just as much fun," she teased.

"Oh, ye of little faith…"

He turned back and tuned out distractions as he lined up his shot. With a flick of his wrist the first ring landed successfully around the neck of a bottle. Erica gasped in surprise. But his second and third ring missed their mark.

"Come on, Morgan. Just two more and the baby gets a bear. Baby needs a bear. No pressure."

He grinned, then cranked up his concentration. The shot was successful. One more and he'd have it made. Taking his time, he did a couple of flicks of his wrist, testing. Then he let the ring go. It wobbled and nearly slid off before firmly settling around the bottle's neck.

"You did it!" In her excitement Erica threw herself into his arms and hugged him.

He pulled her close and breathed in the fresh scent of her hair. Nothing had felt so good in a very long time as this woman did in his arms. He could have held her all night, but too soon she moved away.

"I was wrong about you and not too proud to admit it." She picked out a fluffy brown bear with Harvest Festival embroidered on his paws. Hugging it close she said, "I love this. The baby will, too."

"Maybe mama needs one."

"You're pushing your luck, cowboy."

"Another challenge." And it was a gamble he couldn't back down from. Maybe there was more of his father in him than he wanted to admit. "One more time," he said to the woman, handing over his money.

Five tosses later, Erica was picking out another bear. He carried it as they walked away. "What do you have to say now?"

"You are the king of the carnival games."

"Okay, then."

At the end of the row of booths he stopped and pointed to a sign. "Hayrides. What do you say?"

"I think that sounds like fun."

Her happy smile hit him squarely in the gut and

nearly dropped him to his knees. What was it about this particular woman that made him want to be her hero? She'd said more than once that he was making a habit of bailing her out. He couldn't seem to stop himself. He should be bothered by that and probably would be in the middle of the night when thoughts of her made him toss and turn.

But right now, he was going to sit close to her in a wagon with the moon shining down on them. Playing with fire was dangerous but he couldn't find the will to resist. And if he had the chance to kiss her he wasn't sure he could stop himself.

Chapter Eight

Erica waited a short distance from the hayride while Morgan took the bears he'd won back to his truck. He didn't want them to get mangled or dirty, which was incredibly sweet. And that level of sweetness after a fairly impressive ring toss performance made her realize, not for the first time, that he was a pretty impressive man in so many ways. If things were different maybe...

Nope. Not going there. Wondering "what if" was a waste of time and energy. She was going to be a mother. All the responsibility of taking care of this child would be on her, and she'd reconciled herself to that. Until Morgan, she'd never felt wistful about taking this road alone. She needed to focus on being grateful to be traveling this road at all, because it was impossible to imagine her life without children in it.

"You're still here." Morgan walked up beside her.

Erica had been so lost in thought, she hadn't heard him coming. "I told you I would be."

"One never knows. You hear those stories of an evening gone wrong when a woman heads to the ladies' room and never comes back." His look was wry. "Poor schmuck just sits there until he finally gets it that he's been ditched. And hopes no one noticed."

"First of all, you were the one who left me," she retorted. "Second, I can't wrap my head around any scenario where that has actually happened to you."

"Nope, never has." His expression was casually innocent. Maybe a little too casual?

She put her hand on his arm. "This will either reassure you or feed your ego. But what woman in her right mind would ditch the Harvest Festival ring toss legend?"

"Legend, huh?"

"And ego wins." She tsked. "Don't let it go to your head, cowboy. Your Stetson won't fit."

"Can't a guy just enjoy the moment?" he teased.

"I don't think that's going to be a problem. You're enjoying it quite a lot." She grinned. "But, seriously, that was a pretty awesome accomplishment. My little

Ichabod or Ingrid will be very impressed when he or she is old enough to hear this story."

"Shucks, it was nothing, little lady."

"Not so little, actually. And enough with the B Western cowboy imitation." He was the real deal, not an actor and way more exciting than any of them, she thought. "I was under the impression that we were going on a hayride. But here we are, standing around and talking about you."

"But that's my favorite subject—" He laughed when she playfully slugged him in the arm. "Okay. Let's go. Are you warm enough?"

She had on fur-lined boots, black leggings, a big sweater and a tightly knit fringed poncho over that. "I'm good."

Morgan offered his arm and she slid her hand into the crook of his elbow, liking the feel of him. He was tall and muscular and made her feel feminine and protected, even if it was just for tonight.

Her heart tilted a little and she didn't mind. For right now she wasn't going to question her attraction to him. Or the fact that she wasn't ready to stop touching him when they arrived at the hayride. Over her protest, Morgan paid the man for two tickets.

"A group went out a little while ago," the old guy said. "Should be back any minute. So if you'll just wait over there, I'd be obliged."

"Sure thing." Morgan took her arm and gently steered her to the side. "Don't want to get run over."

"That could ruin a perfectly wonderful evening," she agreed.

"So you're having a good time?"

"Yes." She couldn't remember the last time she'd felt so carefree and content. And just plain happy.

Just then the sound of an approaching tractor drifted to them. The machine rumbled to a stop. It pulled a big wagon with hay bales for seating. The old guy put out a step stool, and once the riders disembarked, he waved the waiting group on.

Morgan jumped up first, then held a hand down to help her. They took their seats and squeezed closer to make more room as others joined them. When the tractor slowly moved forward, it lurched enough to knock Erica into Morgan. He put his arm around her, holding her securely. It felt good, right somehow, and she sighed a little when he didn't let her go.

Smiling up at him, she said, "This is it."

"Ready or not."

She took out her cell phone to snap some pictures of the pumpkin patch they passed. Then the road curved to the right, taking them past Pine Lake, where a nearly full moon left a trail of silver light on the water. It was so beautiful, and she couldn't help thinking romantic, too.

She lifted her phone and snapped another series

of pictures, trying to take a selfie of her and Morgan. Since his reach was longer, he managed to get one.

"Let's see if we broke my camera," she said laughing.

She opened her pictures on the phone. The first one was of the lake, which came out pretty well considering the circumstances. Then she noticed something strange.

"What's this ball of light?"

"Probably just photographic artifact from the flash." Morgan took her phone and looked closely. Then he scrolled to the next picture and said, "Whoa."

Erica gasped. "Now there are three of them. I think they're called orbs. If it's from the flash, why did they multiply?"

"Good question." He scrolled to the next picture and there was just one again. "There's no reason for the change. We're not moving that fast so everything should be about the same."

"I've heard that unexplained lights can be orbs from the spirit world. Light energy. And they often collect around water."

"It's weird for sure. Could just be a coincidence, but—"

"What?" In the moonlight she could see the uneasiness on his face. "Morgan?"

"Daphne Taylor's place is just across the lake."

"The animal sanctuary with resident ghosts?" she clarified.

"Yes," he agreed. "Cue the spooky music. Evan Cruise would love this."

"Who's he?"

"A guy in town who runs ghost tours."

"He should talk to Daphne about her haunted barn." She stared at the pictures. "Maybe these orbs should zip over there, too, and keep her ghost lovers company."

"Are you creeped out?" he asked.

"Yes." She shivered and leaned into him a little more.

His arm tightened around her reassuringly. She looked up and saw an intensity in his eyes that she sensed wasn't about spirit orbs or unexplained phenomena. It had everything to do with her, and their eyes locked in a moment of acute awareness. Everyone around them faded away. It was just him and her.

Slowly he lowered his head and kissed her. The touch was sweet and almost tentative at first, until she moaned softly so that only he could hear. Then it turned into something more, an explosion of attraction that burned away rational thought. She strained for more and he was eager to oblige.

Erica had no idea how long the kiss lasted but suddenly became aware of the steady movement slowing and people around them in the wagon starting to stir.

Morgan lifted his head and glanced around. "I think we're back."

"Yeah—" Erica was in sort of a haze as the tractor slowed even more and came to a stop right where they'd started. "I guess they'll want us to get off."

The other passengers stood there waiting patiently to disembark. In front of her, a woman about her mom's age turned and smiled indulgently at them.

When she noticed Erica looking, she said, "I'm sorry. Don't mean to stare, but you two are just the cutest couple."

"Oh—" She shook her head. "We're very good friends—"

"Even better. Marrying your best friend is a solid foundation for life together. And now you're starting a family." Her gaze dropped to Erica's belly. "And look at you so pregnant and cute. Beautiful expectant mama. Doting dad. And both of you so good-looking. That baby is going to be beautiful." It was her turn to get down from the wagon, and she apologized for holding them up. "Have a good night."

Erica and Morgan were the last to get off, and he helped her down, as carefully as if she were a piece of delicate crystal. His protective attitude hadn't changed, but something else had. She could feel it.

They walked around some more, got something to eat. She chatted about the weather and any other shallow subject that came to mind. He responded in monosyllables. But they carefully avoided discussing the elephant in the room, so to speak.

After seeing all there was to see, they walked back to his truck, and Erica felt an air of tension between them, most of it coming from Morgan. Her teasing friend had disappeared and left a quiet, preoccupied man in his place. She wanted the other guy back, but that would require a conversation. Something told her he wasn't going to raise the subject, so it was up to her.

After he merged the truck into the line of cars exiting the fairgrounds, he turned onto the road leading back to the Ambling A. It was now or never.

"So—" She took a deep breath. "That was awkward. Do you want to talk about it?"

"The kiss?" He gave her a quick glance, then returned his gaze to the road. "Or the woman who assumed I'm the father of your baby?"

She'd been sort of hoping he would grin and say there was nothing to discuss. But she'd given him an opening and he made it bigger. Only a coward would slam it shut now. He'd given her two choices and she picked the latter.

"Does it bother you that people might think you're the baby's father?" She folded her hands in her lap and squeezed them tight.

"If I cared what people thought, I wouldn't have gone to childbirth class with you. People will think what they think. It's a logical conclusion and I don't blame them."

She waited for a "but." It didn't come, and yet his response hadn't relieved the tension. "Who do you blame?"

Instead of answering he asked, "Why isn't the baby's father going with you to the class? Where is he? Shouldn't he be involved?"

In a perfect world, yes, she thought. But this was so far from perfect. She'd decided on a course of action to get what she wanted and would never be sorry for that. No one was going to make her feel like she wasn't enough or that she'd done something she should be ashamed of.

"No," she said. "He shouldn't be involved. I don't need him to be."

"That's a bunch of BS." In the lights from the dash his expression was harsh. "A man takes care of his own if he's any kind of a man."

The words were confirmation that for Morgan being a father was a duty. An obligation. Cleaning up a mess he'd made. And the realization hurt her heart more than it should have.

"Look, Morgan, it's all right if you don't want to be my coach. I understand if it makes you uncomfortable."

"That's not what I'm saying." He didn't raise his voice, which made the words all the more electric. "I said I'd be there and I will. I want to be. I'd just like to know who the father of this baby is. A dead-beat or a jerk?"

For reasons she didn't understand, that made her dig in and pull stubborn around her like a blanket. "That information is on a need-to-know basis, and no one needs to know."

"That kiss says otherwise." Morgan's tone said he had his own brand of stubborn going on.

"I don't think so. Blame it on ghosts and orbs and spirit energy. And that's all I'm going to say about that."

"You're the one who asked if I wanted to talk about it." He turned onto the road leading to the main house on the ranch. "But the truth is *you* don't want to."

"I guess not."

He pulled to a stop at the front door and turned off the engine. "Erica—"

"I had a good time," she said. "Thanks. Good night."

Before he could say more, she got out of the truck and walked inside the house. She leaned her back against the door and held her tears in check. Why was he pushing this? What did it matter? She had walked through fire to have this baby, and he wasn't sure he wanted kids. That was a deal breaker. She had no business even letting it cross her mind that she liked him very much and even less business wishing this thing with them could be more.

It was too bad, really, because she had a feeling they could be good together, that he would be an exceptional husband and father. But he got burned and almost married a woman having another man's baby. Erica's baby would always be another man's. All of that took him out of the need-to-know column about how this baby was conceived.

She didn't think he would take it well and didn't want to find out she was right.

Erica pulled herself together but didn't feel up to putting on a perky face for anyone who might be awake. Still, while living under her parents' roof, she owed them the courtesy of letting them know she was home.

She walked into the great room and found her mother there alone, reading.

"Hi, Mama. I just wanted to let you know I'm home."

Her mother looked up from the book. "Thank you, sweetie."

"Is Daddy in bed?"

"Yes. He was tired." She took off her reading glasses. "How was the Harvest Festival this year?"

"That implies I can compare it to last year, but the truth is that I haven't been there in so long I can't compare it to anything recent."

Her mother closed the book, put it on the table beside her and set her glasses on top of it. "Let me rephrase. Did you have a good time?"

"Yes." Right up until that stranger mistook Morgan for her husband and the father of her baby.

"Did you see anyone there?"

"Of course. The place was packed." But that's not what her mom was asking. All she'd told her folks was her destination. Not the details. Especially that she'd asked Morgan to go. What a brazen hussy, a pregnant brazen hussy. Still, it was one thing to politely follow house rules, quite another to let anyone dictate who she could and couldn't see at thirty years old.

"I went with Morgan Dalton. He picked me up." She glanced down at the stuffed animals in her arms. "He won these playing the ring toss. One for me and one for the baby."

"So, he has skills—"

"Please don't start, Mama."

"That was a joke."

"I'm sorry." She sighed and walked over to sit on the sofa beside her mother, setting the stuffed animals between them. "I guess pregnancy hormones are making me supersensitive."

"I remember. That part is a bitch," her mother said ruefully.

"Language, Mama." She smiled. "But body chemistry does seem to have turned me into one."

Her mother picked up one of the bears and touched the plastic eyes. "These will have to come off. The baby could swallow them."

Erica had already thought of that. Since the pregnancy had been confirmed, she'd been reading everything she could find on child care.

"I'll take care of it," she assured her mother.

"I'm sure you will." Angela put the bear on her lap. "How is everything? Have you heard from the lawyer? Your father said she was going to file suit against Barron Enterprises."

"Yes, she did, but she warned me they can delay the process practically indefinitely and force me to give up."

"But you're made of sterner stuff," her mother said emphatically.

"To a point. But I need a revenue source because the money I have won't last indefinitely." She set the bear down. "I really need a job."

"How's the search going?"

"Nothing so far. I've had some interviews but…" She shrugged. "No one will say it straight out that they don't want to hire me because I'm pregnant. That would be discrimination. But… It's discouraging. I feel as if I'm stuck until after the baby is born. And it's a catch 22. I want to settle in a place of my own for the baby. But I don't feel comfortable doing that until I have cash flow again. I'm sorry that I'm putting you and Daddy out."

"Are you kidding?" Her mother glanced around the large room. "This place is huge. And we love you. You're welcome to stay here as long as you want."

She caught the corner of her lip between her teeth. "But I can't help thinking—"

"What?" Apparently sensitivity hormones were just waiting to pounce, because they kicked up again. "If only I had a husband?"

"No, sweetie. I wasn't going to say that. If only someone could see past the pregnancy. Someone who knows how smart and determined you are. You'd be an asset anywhere you worked if they could see their way clear to give you an opportunity. Those bozos are thinking short-term and that's their loss."

"Thanks, Mama." The words were encouraging and made her want to explain why she was in this situation. "I'd hoped to find a husband. That perfect someone. Get married, then have a baby right away before my eggs get old and dry up like raisins." She shook her head. "It just never happened. You were lucky with Daddy."

"I know it. He's a keeper."

Erica thought she'd found that with Peter, until she mentioned having children and they broke up. The thing was, there'd been no hole in her life when he was gone. In a lot of ways it had been a relief. She'd put in so much energy, and maybe that was just about trying to make it work because her biological clock was ticking.

Shouldn't caring about someone be effortless? The feelings just there? Like with Morgan. The thought popped into her mind and stuck. She wondered if they might have had a chance if it wasn't for the baby. But there was still the question of having kids at all. If she fell for him, it would land her in the same boat as she'd been with Peter.

"I need you to know something, Mama."

"What, sweetie?"

"Do you remember how much I loved my dolls when I was a little girl?"

"Of course." She smiled and looked as if she was pulling up those long-ago memories. "Your daddy built you that dollhouse and little furniture for your babies."

"Is it still in that storage shed in the barn?"

"As far as I know."

"Good." She pressed her palms to her belly. "I'll want to get it out if this baby is a girl."

"Absolutely." There was a soft expression in her mother's eyes. "I know there are all kinds of urban myths about how to tell the sex of a baby, and you'll think I'm being silly, but—"

"I'd never think that."

"You're carrying this baby a lot like I did you. With Gabe I was all out front. Daddy teased that it looked like I had a basketball under my shirt. From the back you couldn't tell I was pregnant."

Erica laughed. "And with me?"

"I seemed to spread out."

"Pretty soon I'll need a warning sign that says Wide Load."

"Hardly. You look healthy and beautiful."

"You're just prejudiced, Mama."

"Of course I am. You're my baby. I love being your mother. And I wanted more babies." Something flashed in her eyes. Something distant, sad and painful.

"I remember how much you did. And the miscarriages."

Angela linked her fingers around the teddy bear she still held and pressed it close to her body. "I had you and Gabe two years apart and it was hard, emotionally and physically. When you were a little older, a bit more independent, I realized I wanted more children."

"I've never forgotten the heartbreak you went through trying to have another baby," Erica said. "And now I understand, because I feel the same way. How you'd move heaven and earth just to feel that sweet warm body in your arms. And because of what happened, you should appreciate better than anyone why my life would not feel complete without a child. And why it's so important for me to do it now. Because I'm the same age you were when—"

"I get it." Still, there was a question in her mother's eyes although she didn't say more.

"I promised myself that if I was fortunate enough to get pregnant, I was having the baby. No matter what. Because later could be too late."

Angela sighed and nodded, but didn't say more or ask any questions. Talking about that painful time was hard for her, but opening up even just a little made Erica feel closer to her mother than she had in a very long time. The mother-daughter bond had suffered in the past twelve years. She took responsibility for that, and tonight was another small step toward fixing it.

She could feel how much her mom wanted her to talk about the baby's father, but now even more than before she was afraid to go there. If she confessed that she'd gone to a sperm bank, it could set their fragile bond back, even make it irreparable. And she couldn't do that. Wouldn't do that.

Neither of them broke the silence. But her mother still held that bear.

Finally she smiled. "So, you had a good time with Morgan?"

"Yes. He's fun."

"I'm glad. You've had a lot to deal with lately, and there's nothing wrong with having some fun." She glanced up. "And it's important that you're comfortable with the person who's going to coach you through labor."

The truth was she did feel comfortable with him, and he was the only one she felt that way about since coming back. She wasn't sure why she'd refused to explain to him how the baby was conceived. Maybe it was because she hadn't been ready for the question. Or she was afraid of how he would react. That's what happened when your feelings became more than they should be.

Whatever the reason, she needed to tell him the truth. As soon as possible.

Chapter Nine

A few days after the Harvest Festival, Morgan was mucking out stalls in the barn. As the oldest brother he probably could have delegated to one of the others, but the crappy job suited his crappy mood. He hadn't talked to Erica since dropping her off that night and didn't much like the way they'd left things. It didn't make him happy, but he missed her. And he was ticked off. Mad at himself for pushing. Mad at her for stonewalling him. He chucked a pitchfork full of hay and muck into the wheelbarrow beside him with more force than was necessary.

He was also mad that the evening had been ruined. He'd been having a really good time, the best since moving to Bronco. Kissing Erica was a particularly memorable highlight. Her lips were soft and eager. Her sexy, throaty sounds said she liked it, too. Then it all went sideways with that lady's comments.

Truth was, Erica was carrying another man's child. Yet all she would say was that the father wasn't an issue and Morgan didn't need to know more.

That kiss said he did and was the reason he couldn't let go of the questions. Did the father know about the baby? Did he not care? What if he had a change of heart and came after her? What if she had a change of heart and wanted to make it work with him?

Another pile of muck went in the wheelbarrow. That was followed by a string of language that made him glad he wasn't a kid anymore with his mother standing there holding a bar of soap to wash out his mouth.

He really liked Erica. It was why he'd offered to help her. But things were changing; feelings were shifting. Getting complicated. He was confused and didn't know what he wanted. But he was crystal clear that he didn't want to keep stumbling around in the dark and get blindsided by another man. He intended to see Erica through the birth of that baby, but before the next class they needed to have a chat.

Morgan heard voices and one of them was a woman's. He looked up and saw Erica coming into the barn with his father. That man being around her tweaked his already bad attitude. He rested the pitch-fork against the stall's fence and stepped into the opening, watching the two of them walk down the center aisle toward him. She was smiling at something Neal Dalton said and Morgan felt the knot in his gut pull tighter.

His father noticed him there. "Hey, son."

He wanted to say he didn't need the reminder about their shared DNA. But he didn't, not in front of Erica.

"Look who's here," Neal said.

Erica smiled a little tentatively, not her usual, bright wattage cheerful expression. "Hi, Morgan."

"Hey."

"Watch your step," his father said, putting a protective hand under her elbow. "Don't want you falling, or stepping in something."

She laughed. "I'm a ranch kid. Grew up in the barn. I used to ride all the time, but that's on hold for now."

"Deb, my wife, loves to ride. After her heart attack, I got a little overprotective about her on a horse." His expression was teasing, but there was worry around the edges. "She wasn't a happy camper. And that's an understatement. Right, Morgan?"

"Yeah." His curt answer got a raised eyebrow from Erica.

Neal noticed but overlooked it and kept up the charm crusade in front of a pretty woman. "She followed doctor's orders to exercise and change her diet. Dinner isn't as exciting these days, but she's more important to me than carbs and cream sauce."

"So, she's all right now?" Erica asked.

"She is. Me and the boys are making sure of it. She put a scare into all of us." His amiable, easygoing grin disappeared. "I honestly don't know what I'd do without that woman."

"Hopefully you won't have to find out. And she's lucky to have you," Erica said.

Morgan's scoffing sound earned him another sharp look from her, but his father ignored it. After a year of working together, the man had apparently gotten used to his attitude and met it with gruffness. Morgan made no secret of how he felt and let the man deal with it however he wanted.

"No. I'm the lucky one." Neal met her gaze with a remarkably sincere look, then said, "Okay. I'll let you two talk."

"It was nice to see you, Mr. Dalton."

"Neal. Please." He politely touched the brim of his Stetson. "The pleasure is mine, Erica."

In silence they watched him walk away. Morgan knew there was a fine line between charm, flirting and just plain friendliness. He wasn't sure which side of that line his father had just walked, but women usually had a sense of those things and Erica seemed fine. He, Morgan, was the one she apparently had an issue with.

When they were alone, she said, "I know you're working. I hope I'm not interrupting."

He gave her an "oh please" look. "Yeah, because shoveling dirty hay takes a lot of concentration."

"I'll take that as a no." She twisted her fingers together. "So, your dad is nice."

"That's a matter of opinion."

"I know you told me your parents had problems, but I just saw them together. They were like newlyweds."

"Yeah." He took off his work gloves and shoved them in the back pocket of his jeans.

"How long ago was your mother's heart attack?"

"Before we moved here."

"You came for her, but why do you stay?" Her eyes narrowed. "Clearly you resent your father. I know ranch work. It's not like you can avoid him. My father and brother have a really good relationship. But Daddy is set in his ways. He and Gabe get into it when my brother comes up with some 'newfangled' ideas. My brother rebelled in his own way by backing off and getting into real estate."

Morgan thought about his recent negotiations with the man. "I don't know about real estate, but he can wheel and deal pretty well when stock is involved."

"My point is that he distanced himself from conflict and you put yourself into the middle of it. Why don't you go?"

"I stay for my mom. She wanted her family back

together, and I won't be the one to break it up. We all want to take care of her."

"That's sweet." Erica's eyes grew soft. "You're probably not going to like this, but you remind me a lot of your father. In a good way. I can see where you get your charming streak."

"I'm nothing like him." Morgan did his best to push back against the bad. But her words gave him an opening. "You're probably not going to like this. But we all have DNA. From our mothers and fathers. The baby you're carrying is no different. You know what I'm asking, and I'd appreciate it if you didn't tell me again that I don't need to know."

"I don't plan to," she said. "That's actually why I'm here. To tell you about the baby's father."

"Are you in love with him?" Morgan surprised himself with the question. He hadn't planned to ask, but the words were just right there and he couldn't stop them.

Erica blinked at him, then started laughing.

He'd expected anger or indignation, not this. "What's so damn funny?"

Her amusement faded slowly and she got serious. "There is no father—well, not like *that*. I went to a sperm bank."

He moved closer and badly wanted to touch her, but he'd been doing a dirty job and kept his hands to himself. He also wouldn't stop this flow of information. "That's not an easy thing to do on your own, Erica. If you want to talk about it, I'm happy to listen."

She nodded. "It would be a relief actually."

He angled his head toward the other side of the barn. "There's a bench over there. Something tells me this isn't going to be fast."

"Probably not—" Then she stopped and looked unsure. "But you're working. I don't want to bother you."

"Trust me—the stalls will still be there after I take a break."

"Okay." She fell into step beside him, and they stopped at the wooden bench, then sat side by side.

He met her gaze. "I'm listening."

"I dated someone in Denver. Peter. He's the son of the owner of the media company where I worked." She looked down for a moment at the clasped hands in her lap. "Things were getting serious and I thought marriage was the next step. It seemed as if we wanted all the same things—until I brought up kids."

"I take it he was a no vote?"

"Yup. And that was a roadblock for me. So we broke up."

Morgan studied her and decided she didn't seem too upset about it. So he stayed quiet and let her go on.

She told him how loud her biological clock was ticking, how she was pushing thirty and fearing the fertility issues her mother had faced at that age. How she felt it was now or never.

"Never, for me, wasn't an option. So, I went the sperm bank route. Got lucky on my first round of insemination."

Morgan saw a look on her face, part anger, part disillusionment. "There's more, isn't there?"

"Yeah. Peter started dating a receptionist at the company not long after we split. I wasn't at all hurt. Figured I dodged a bullet. But they got married and she was pregnant."

"That had to have hit a nerve," he said.

"I'm not going to lie. It did, but even that was okay. I didn't love him, and I was over the moon about having a baby." But not everything went well, she told him, when Peter's father gave her the ultimatum: transfer to Miami or get fired. She shrugged. "And here I am."

"That sucks." He heard how that sounded. "Not that you're here, but the way it happened," he clarified.

"I knew what you meant." When she looked at him, there was uncertainty in her expression. "This experience of becoming a mother isn't going at all as I planned."

"I'm really sorry you went through that. But I can't say I'm sorry to hear that some guy isn't going to turn up and arm-wrestle me to be your labor coach."

"Nope, that's not going to happen." She grinned, but wariness erased it. "But this is why I can't say anything to my folks. Daddy can't even embrace new and improved ranching techniques. I don't think the idea of a sperm bank grandbaby would go over well."

"I can see why you're hesitant. But you were the one who said we should give our families a chance."

"You first," she said.

"Touché." He laughed, then turned serious. "So you weren't in love with Peter."

"No." She caught the corner of her lip between her teeth, and uncertainly met his gaze. "Are you still in love with the girl you bought the ring for?"

"I thought I was at the time. Looking back, I don't think I ever really loved her."

And speaking of love… Morgan was awfully damn glad Erica wasn't in love with her baby's father. But that meant his feelings were turning into more than he wanted them to be. If it was anyone else, he'd walk away, but after giving his word to see her through the birth, he wouldn't back out. It would be okay, though, he reasoned. It wouldn't be long until the baby was born. He'd keep his promise, then that would be that.

The morning after clearing the air with Morgan, Erica was both relieved and full of purpose. He didn't resign as her coach. That made her unreasonably happy. Also, crying on Mel's shoulder about her job search turned out to be not all bad. She'd come up with an idea and was energized.

She'd interviewed with perfect strangers who could only see her pregnancy. They knew that shortly after starting she would be absent for six weeks. So, she needed to talk to someone who *did* know her.

It was barely nine o'clock, and she was in her room because privacy was required for the call she was about to make. And she had a strategy. She wanted to catch Jordan Taylor just as the workday started, before he was up to his neck in Taylor Beef business. After tapping in the number on her cell phone, she waited.

But she didn't get further than the receptionist.

"I'm sorry. Mr. Taylor's busy today and asked me to hold his calls. But I'll make sure and give him a message."

The woman was friendly but firm. Erica knew assertiveness was almost certainly not going to work in her favor. So, she could leave the darn message, then go camp out at his office and be the proverbial squeaky wheel. It was incredibly irritating, but the woman was simply doing her job.

Erica would admit to the tiniest bit of prejudice toward anyone in that position. Based on the fact that a receptionist at Barron Enterprises was responsible for putting her in need of a job, she had a right to the feeling.

"A message would be great." She repeated her

name, recited her phone number and said to tell him that she was back in town and would like to say hello.

She ended the call and thought about her next move to contact the man she'd gone out with all those years ago. She'd never felt they'd clicked romantically and apparently neither had Jordan. One night he'd told her he liked her, but she felt more like his little sister than his girlfriend and he hoped they could still be friends. Then they'd had a nice dinner together. It was the best brush-off she'd ever had.

Since then she'd run into him on visits home over the years, and Jordan had always been friendly. At least that's how she saw it. Hopefully he did, too, and would give her a chance to prove she had a lot to offer his company if he could see his way past the pregnancy.

Her stomach rumbled, reminding her that she hadn't eaten yet this morning. She needed fuel for this job-hunting campaign and went downstairs to the kitchen. Malone was the only one in the room.

"Mornin'," he said.

"Same to you." She looked around. "Where's Mama?"

"She left early. Said she had shopping to do. Something about a new dress for that Denim and Diamonds shindig."

"Right."

A wave of mixed feelings washed over Erica. On the one hand, with all the tension in the house right now it was kind of a relief not to see her mom. Their one talk after the Harvest Festival had made things better but hadn't completely resolved the strain. On the other hand, she missed the time when they would have made a day of buying a special occasion dress, then gone to lunch. She missed that so much.

"Are you hungry?" Malone looked at her baby bump. "Gotta feed that little one. And before you say anything, I know you're not eating for two. You don't have to double your rations."

It surprised her that he knew about not doubling up on calories when you were pregnant. "I am starving, actually."

"Okay. I can whip up some pancakes and eggs. Got some fruit cut up. Now sit. I'll have breakfast ready in a jiffy."

"And I can have one cup of coffee."

Caffeine wasn't strictly forbidden during pregnancy, but limiting it was recommended.

She did as he instructed, and he put a mug of steaming coffee in front of her. Then he proceeded to mix the pancake batter. While she watched, her cell phone rang and the ID said Private. She hoped this was who she thought it was.

As soon as she heard his voice, she knew it was.

"Hi, Jordan. You got my message." And he was returning her call a lot faster than she'd expected. Hopefully that was a good sign.

"Yes, you caught my receptionist when she was

actually working." Oddly, there was a smile in his voice. "So, you're back. Are you home to stay?"

"Yes. And that's kind of what I wanted to talk to you about."

"Okay. I have a meeting now but I'd really like to catch up. Could you meet me for lunch?"

"That would be great, Jordan. Tell me where and when." After he gave her the information, she said, "Okay. See you then."

She ended the call and saw Malone looking at her. "What?"

"That's what I'd like to know." He poured batter on the griddle and scrambled eggs into a skillet.

"I'm just meeting an old friend for lunch. I have to feed the baby, right?"

"And this old friend just happens to be the one your folks were hoping you'd end up at the altar with." That wasn't disapproval in his voice. Not exactly.

"Yes. Why?"

"He's got a reputation with women. Quantity, not quality, or so I've heard."

"It's not like that with us," she assured him. "Besides, look at me." She glanced down at her very rounded belly. "I'm so not his type."

"Still—" He finished cooking, then slid pancakes and eggs onto a plate and carried it to her at the table, along with a bowl of fruit.

"You're sweet to worry about me, but there's no

need." She was the one who wanted something from Jordan.

Which was why a few hours later she got to DJ's Deluxe and told the hostess she was meeting someone. The woman pointed him out and Erica walked over to the table where he was already seated. He stood as she approached and his eyes widened, evidence that he noticed her condition.

He gave her a hug and kissed her cheek, then held her at arm's length. "Look at you."

"Yup." She smiled. "Gonna be a mom."

"I didn't know you were married."

"I'm not."

He studied her for several moments, then simply said, "Congratulations."

"Thank you." She sat down across from him. "It's been a while. How are you, Jordan?"

"Good."

"And your dad?"

He shook his head slightly. "Same as always."

She saw a look in his eyes and said no more. The man who intimidated her also had a reputation for being difficult, and she couldn't imagine being his son. But not everything was his cross to bear. He was very tall and very handsome, with short dark hair and brown eyes that were incredibly compelling. A man that women noticed. He was also the son of the richest man in town, and women noticed that, too.

"What's new?" she asked.

"Not much." He shrugged those broad shoulders. "But you've got a lot going on. A baby on the way. Miss Independent moving back to Bronco Heights. Why?"

"Because I got fired from my job in Denver." There was no point in evading. They'd always been honest with each other, and she wasn't about to be anything less now. She told him the whole humiliating story, except for the part about how she got pregnant. Then she explained about filing a lawsuit against her previous employer.

"I think your attorney is right that you've got a good case."

Their server walked over then, and they ordered.

When he was gone, Jordan met her gaze. "How can I help, Erica?"

"I was hoping you'd ask." She leaned forward. "I need a job. The money I've saved won't last forever, and this lawsuit could take a long time to resolve."

"I see."

"I realize this is presuming on our friendship, but no one in their right mind will hire a woman in the third trimester of pregnancy."

"It's touchy," he admitted.

"I have upper management experience and a lot to offer. If you give me an opportunity, I promise you won't regret it."

"Of course I can help." He didn't even hesitate. "We're always looking for good people."

"Really? Just like that," she said.

"It's the least I can do for a friend. But I have a feeling you'll be doing me a favor in the long run." He took out his cell phone and started tapping into it. "I'm texting my assistant now to check my schedule and then she'll contact you to make an appointment to come by."

Her eyes got a little blurry with grateful tears, but she blinked several times, determined not to get emotional. "I don't know how to thank you."

"Name the baby after me. Jordan works for a girl or a boy."

His teasing smile brought women to their knees, but she was immune. Why was that? Because she had that reaction to another man. Every time she saw Morgan, her heart skipped a beat and her legs wobbled a little. It made her wonder about what combination of factors attracted a certain woman to a certain man.

Before she could decide, their food arrived and she couldn't believe she was hungry again after the big breakfast she'd eaten. Now that the reason for this meeting had been settled, she could relax and enjoy catching up. They reminisced about the short time they'd dated and decided it wasn't a total waste, what with the friendship that came out of it.

She speared a piece of chicken and lettuce. "You know my parents were hoping I'd fall for you and not go away to college."

"Really?" He took a sip of his beer. "I don't think you ever told me that."

"It's true. They wanted me to marry you. Home-town boy."

"Sorry to disappoint," he teased.

"Unless I miss my guess, I think they're still holding on just a little bit to some kind of fantasy that we'll see the error of our ways and get married." She laughed, then looked up from her salad, expecting that he would be laughing, too.

He wasn't. And his expression was a little dark and brooding. "You deserve someone better than me, Erica."

"Don't be ridiculous."

"I don't think I am. I'm not good enough for you." He looked thoughtful. "And you're going to have a baby. That's a special responsibility."

"The fact that you recognize it as such is proof that you're so much better than you think you are."

He shook his head. "You're wrong."

Erica disagreed, but trying to convince him of that would be a waste of time. There was no question that he was flawed, but who wasn't? She considered him a good friend. And she was confident he was a good man.

As good as Morgan?

Since when was he the bar by which she judged other men? Maybe it was talking about the responsibility of a baby that made her think of him now.

It was a darn shame that he didn't want kids and doubted his suitability as a father.

She liked him very much and that kiss at the Harvest Festival said he liked her, too. But this baby had to be her first priority. Sometimes liking someone a lot just wasn't enough.

Chapter Ten

Talking to Jordan the day before had eased Erica's stress level by a lot. As promised, his assistant had called to make an appointment for the following week. He'd assured her there would be a job after the baby was born, and in all the years she'd known him, he'd never lied to her. There was no reason to believe he was now. That morning she'd visited Gramps and tried to coax him to talk. Sadly he didn't say anything. After lunch she was at loose ends and the waiting without anything to fill her time was driving her nuts. She was used to being busy.

Between Malone cooking and hired help with the housekeeping, her mother didn't need any assistance.

So, Erica wandered down to the barn to see what her father was up to. She walked inside and found him cleaning out stalls. The last time she'd seen Morgan, he was doing the same thing. Not too proud to handle a dirty job. Just like her father.

"Hi, Daddy. Don't you pay people to do this?"

He looked up from shoveling horse manure into a wheelbarrow. "It's relaxing. Keeps me from thinking too much." She was probably a big part of what he didn't want to think about. But burying his head in the sand wasn't going to change anything, and she wanted to do what she could to repair their relationship. "I'm looking for something to do to earn my keep. Can I give you a hand with this?"

He frowned at her. "Don't you need to take it easy? With the baby?"

"The doctor says to do whatever I've been doing. Except riding horses. Can't risk a fall."

"Yeah. I remember that from when your mama was pregnant with Gabe and you." He smiled, remembering something. "She's pretty stubborn and missed riding. It was awfully tempting to get on a horse. Lucky she had me to keep her honest."

The subtext of that was Erica had no one. Well, she had herself and was doing all the right things for her health and the baby's. And she had Morgan to help her through the birth. Just thinking about him brought a blush to her face. It was involuntary because if she had any control, it wouldn't happen.

She refused to think about what their relationship would be after the baby was born. Day-to-day survival was her priority now and she didn't have to worry about a job. Everything was falling into place, so she refused to let her father's comment bother her.

"How about you let me sweep up when you finish that part. And I can spread out clean hay. If you lift the bale, I'll just walk back and forth with the pitchfork. Think of it as getting my daily exercise."

"Sounds okay to me." He smiled at her. It was almost the way he used to before she decided to have a baby by herself.

They worked in silence for a while and then Erica asked, "Do you think about retiring, Daddy?"

"Why would I?"

"Running a ranch is a lot of work."

"And if I don't do it, who will?" He shoveled more muck, then met her gaze through the fence dividing the stalls.

"Gabe will."

"I suppose." He leaned on the shovel. "If he doesn't have me to contend with, he can do it his way. We don't see eye to eye on how to run things these days. I don't see any good reason to change. This land has been in the family for generations and we're doing just fine. Your brother is into his real estate deals. That's *his* way of pushing back."

If Erica was the sensitive type, she would have bristled at that remark. As if her having a baby without marriage and a husband was her preferred rebellion strategy. But, again, she made a conscious effort to let that roll off her back.

"What did Gabe want to do that was so revolutionary?"

Her father stopped working and pushed his Stetson off his forehead a little as he thought about the question and looked down at the wheelbarrow. "Well, take this for instance."

"Horse poop?"

"Yeah." He grinned. "He had me read an article and the title was 'What to do with poo.'"

"Catchy." She laughed. "You compost this, right? And spread it in the pasture?"

"We do. But there's something called manure share."

"Do I even want to know about this?" she asked.

"Probably safer than talking about other things," he said, looking down at her belly. "It's a program that connects livestock owners who have excess manure with gardeners, landscapers and large scale composters. According to your brother, it benefits the environment and the economy of local communities."

"Call me crazy, Daddy, but that sounds like a good program."

"Maybe." He didn't look convinced. "But I've got better things to do than coordinate poo pickups."

"I think you're just being stubborn."

"Takes one to know one," he said pointedly.

She ignored that and pitched more hay on the stall floor. "We're talking about you now."

"Okay. I think the terms old-fashioned and set in my ways have been thrown out more than once to describe me." He met her gaze. "There's probably some truth in it."

"They say recognizing a problem is halfway to solving it."

"I never said I had a problem. If it's not broke, don't fix it, I always say. When I'm not running things, this operation will change. And someday this land will belong to Gabe and you and my grandchildren—" He didn't finish the thought, and the silence was—well—pregnant.

She walked over to the opening of the stall next to hers where he was working. "What is it, Daddy? Something other than the obvious is bothering you. Please talk to me."

He looked at her. "The baby you're carrying is my grandchild. Mine and your mother's. It's something we've looked forward to and prayed would happen for a long time now. We've worked hard for all these years to know that everything will pass on to another generation of Abernathys. Whether you want to talk about him or not, that baby has a father. What if he turns up demanding visitation and more? Some cockamamie claim on the Ambling A?"

"That won't happen," she assured him. "I guarantee it."

"How can you? There are stories on the news all the time about courts granting property and all kinds of demands to someone with flimsy paternity claims."

Her father had just admitted he was set in his ways and had no use for new techniques. Her pregnancy via anonymous sperm donation would, in his mind, fall in that category. This was the absolute wrong time to explain how she could be so certain that no one was going to show up and demand anything.

"You're just going to have to trust me, Daddy."

She went back to the stall where she'd been working and finished spreading the hay. Her father didn't say much more, and the awkward silence persisted. More than once it crossed her mind to leave him alone, but there was a lot of truth to that stubborn Abernathy streak. She stuck it out until the job was finished.

Afterward, Erica want back to the main house, left her dirty boots on the back porch then went up to her room to shower away barn dust. She'd thought the spray of warm water would relax her after the conversation with her father, but it didn't. She was still feeling a little raw.

On her way to the stairs she passed her parents'

room and noticed her mother was there, looking at something on the bed. "Mama?"

"Erica. Come on in."

She walked inside the large room and went directly to the king-size, cherrywood sleigh bed.

"Is that your dress?" She looked down at a fancy gown laid out on the duvet. "This is for Denim and Diamonds?"

"Yes." Her mother picked up the hanger and held the dress up in front of her. It was a long-sleeved black sheath with gorgeous beading. "What do you think?"

"It's just beautiful, Mama." She smiled. "That's going to look fabulous on you."

"You don't think it's too young for me?"

"No way. It's classic. Elegant. And besides, you aren't old. Unless it's a miniskirt and boots, you can pull off anything."

"Okay. Good." Her mother sighed. "I just love it, too. So, what about jewelry?"

"It is Denim and Diamonds after all. Don't you have some big, honkin' diamond earrings that Daddy bought you for a significant birthday?"

"Yes. They'd be perfect." Her mother walked to the mirror over the dresser, held the gown up in front of her and assessed the look. She beamed a satisfied smile.

"You're going to be the belle of the ball, Mama."

It felt really good to just talk girl stuff. No undercurrents. Just enjoying feminine conversation.

"It should be something," her mother agreed. She walked over to Erica and started to say something, then pressed her lips tightly together. "So, Malone tells me you had a call from Jordan. Unless you know another one, I assume that's Jordan Taylor?"

"Yes. I had lunch with him yesterday."

"Oh?" Her mother's eyes gleamed with interest. "And?"

"He looks good."

"Of course he does. They don't call him Bronco's most eligible bachelor for nothing." She waited a moment, then prodded a little. "So you just stared at a nice-looking man over a table at lunch?"

"Funny." Erica grinned. "We did some catching up."

"Is he seeing anyone?"

"He didn't say, so the answer to that question is either no or nothing serious."

The gleam in her mother's eyes intensified. It was a spark of hope. "I guess he noticed that you're pregnant."

"Yes. He congratulated me." And didn't ask any questions, which she appreciated.

"Did you make plans to see each other again?" Angela asked.

"As a matter of fact, we did." She was going to hell, but Erica couldn't resist leading her mother on a bit. Served her right for not letting this go.

"Lunch again? Or maybe dinner?"

"I have an appointment to talk to him about a job."

"And?"

"That's it. He said they're always looking for talented people at Taylor Beef, and he was sure there was something for me."

Her mother looked a little startled. "But you're going to have a baby."

"That's not a news flash, Mama. And that's why I really need a job."

"There's no need to rush into anything, Erica. This is your home."

"I appreciate that. More than I can say. But—"

"But nothing. What will you do with the baby after it's born?"

"I'll find child care."

"Babies need their mothers."

"And I will take care of him or her," Erica protested. "Part of that is earning a living so I can support us."

"Like I said, you have a home. Your father and I can take care of you both—"

"Mama, please don't take this wrong. But I only moved in here temporarily. To get on my feet. I appreciate you and Daddy letting me come home so I can do that. Once the baby's born and I'm back at work, I'll find a place for us to live."

"I suppose I can't talk you out of that."

"If I hadn't been fired, that's what I'd be doing in Denver. It was always my plan, Mama."

"I see." Her mother walked past her to the closet. Without turning, she said, "I need to hang this up, then I've got some things to do."

Erica had seen tears in her eyes and heard the break of emotion in her voice. She started to say something, then stopped. It wouldn't do any good. Angela Abernathy had never come to terms with her daughter going away to school, then having a career somewhere so far from home. Being a ranch wife and mother was her career, and she didn't understand Erica's choices any more than her father accepted new ranching ideas. This wasn't the time to point out that at least she would be living close by this time.

Still she felt awful. She didn't want to hurt her parents, but she had to live life on her own terms. She'd kept intending to tell them about the baby but put it off. Maybe in the back of her mind she believed if they held their newborn grandchild and bonded, the circumstances wouldn't be a big deal.

Women plan, God laughs. But she didn't think this was funny. The only thing getting her through was Morgan. They had childbirth class tonight and she would see him. She was looking forward to that very much.

"So, Erica is picking you up again this evening?" Deborah Dalton toyed with the mug of coffee in front of her.

"Yeah." Morgan sat at the round, oak table in his

kitchen, eating the stew his mother had brought over. Her excuse was that she always fixed too much, and that was probably partly true. The other part was, feeding him was a way to stay connected. Better known as pumping him for information.

He figured her question was just the beginning of an inquisition. The innocent expression on her still-beautiful face was a dead giveaway.

"Erica insists on it," he said.

"Usually a gentleman picks up a lady for a date."

"It's not a date, Mom. She says I'm doing her a favor. The least she can do is drive."

His mother looked down for a second, then met his gaze again. "Why *did* you agree to be her labor coach?"

"Actually I offered. She's going through a lot and I can help. That's it." He shrugged.

"But having a baby is an intimate and emotional experience."

One that should be shared with the father of said baby. His mother didn't say that straight out, but it was there all the same. He wished the woman would get off this subject, and he planned to make that happen. "Cops and firefighters and regular civilians deliver babies for perfect strangers all the time. Not that I'm delivering it, but... She's my friend. It's the least I can do."

"You really like her." That wasn't a question.

It was a different subject and he was even less comfortable talking about this one. "As a friend."

"Erica told me that your kindness and sensitivity are the first things she noticed about you."

"I'm a hell of a guy."

"Just like your father." Her unwavering look was a dare for him to convince her she was wrong about the man's character.

Morgan tried to resist the challenge, but just couldn't. "I'm not like him."

She shot an exasperated look in his direction. "There's no getting around the science. He's your father. You have his DNA—the good, bad and handsome. It's been thirty-five years and he still makes my heart flutter and my knees weak."

"I don't want to know that, Mom." He did not like where this conversation was going.

"Tough. If I can forgive him, so can you."

"That's where you're wrong." He loved his mother a lot. He'd do anything for her and proved that when he moved to Dalton's Grange because she'd explained how important it was to her. None of that meant his attitude toward his father had or ever would change.

"Morgan, we're all only human. We have flaws. You. Me. And your father. People don't always make the best choices when they're under stress. That doesn't mean we should disregard the positive parts of them."

"You made your choice. You have to live with

him," he allowed. "I just have to work with him." He buttered one of the biscuits she baked and took a bite. It melted in his mouth. "These are really good."

"Your father said the same thing." Again the challenge was in her eyes for him to deny the connection.

"There isn't anyone on the planet who wouldn't like these. Don't give me that look," he said.

"Okay. Suit yourself. But don't expect me to stop trying."

"Suit yourself. It's your time to waste." He would do almost anything for this woman, but letting his father off the hook wasn't one of them. "I love you, Mom."

"I know. And I love you, too. Even though you're stubborn like your father. Although, in all fairness, you get it from both sides. Truthfully, I'm not sure whether or not that's a flaw."

"I'm not stubborn," he said. "It's just that I'm always right."

She rolled her eyes. "When did you say Erica is coming?"

"About a half hour." Morgan was keeping a close watch on the time and planned to be outside waiting, so she didn't have to come up to the door and knock.

"I'll get out of here before that. Otherwise she'll think I lied about you living with your mother."

"Maybe I should hire you to cook," he teased.

"You couldn't afford me." Her grin was equal parts confidence and self-satisfaction.

She got up and washed the casserole dish she'd brought the food in. Then she said goodbye and headed to the door. Just before she opened it, there was a knock.

"She's really early," Morgan said.

"Hmm." His mother opened it. "Erica. Hi."

"Hello." If she was surprised, it didn't show. "Nice to see you, Mrs. Dalton."

"Oh please. Call me Deborah. Better yet Deb."

"Okay. Thanks. Is Morgan—"

"I'm here." He moved beside his mom. "Come in. It's cold outside."

"Thanks."

"You're really early. I was going to wait for you outside so you didn't have to get out of the car."

"Oh—" She looked first at his mom, then him. "Sorry. I was ready and didn't want to wait around."

He saw tension in her eyes and the set of her mouth. "Is something wrong?"

"No. At least nothing new."

"Come and sit down," his mom said. "And tell us what's bothering you."

"There's plenty of time before the class," he assured her.

She hesitated for several moments, then sighed and nodded. After walking over to the leather sofa, she sat and he settled beside her. Not as close as he wanted to be.

His mother took one of the chairs and set the

empty casserole dish on the matching ottoman. "Okay. How can we help?"

Erica's smile was rueful and sad. "Just don't click your heels three times and say 'there's no place like home.' Or 'you can't go home again.' I found that out."

"That would mean there's no positive movement with your family," he guessed.

She shook her head. "I tried. I was hanging out with my dad in the barn. Helping him. Earning my keep. But he's stubborn."

"There's a lot of that going around." Morgan met his mom's gaze and saw sympathy in her eyes.

"Right." She twisted her fingers together in her lap. "And my mother—" She looked at Deborah. "We were so close before I went to Colorado."

"Letting go of her children is hard on a mother. Especially when they go far away."

Morgan didn't miss the message in his mother's eyes. She wasn't above using her not so long ago health crisis to bring her sons together.

"Well, now I'm back," Erica said. "With a baby on board. But I'm not married, and that's not the way they wanted to be grandparents."

"Oh, honey—" His mother made a sympathetic sound. "They'll come around."

"I don't think so. Apparently I made another mistake." She looked down for a second. "I had the audacity to look for a job. I contacted Jordan Taylor."

She told them about Jordan's promise to find her a position at Taylor Beef.

Morgan had heard about the guy. A newcomer picked up a lot of information hanging out at DJ's Deluxe bar. He'd heard about Jordan Taylor's reputation with the ladies. "Isn't that the guy your folks wanted you to marry?"

"Yes. Even today Mama was hoping and hinting there might still be a chance with him. The thing is, she said I don't need a job because they can take care of me and the baby." She clasped her hands so tightly her knuckles turned white. "I don't want that. It's my responsibility to support us. My mother's always been a ranch wife. She doesn't understand that I want to do it on my own. And I can."

His mother's expression was kind and concerned. "Women have hard decisions to make when it comes to family and career. I know all about that."

"Really?" Erica's eyes widened.

She nodded. "Before I met my husband, I was a career woman. On my way to top-tier management. Or possibly the first female president of the company."

"Wow. What happened?"

"Neal Dalton happened." She got a soft look on her face and shrugged. "I was a city girl and met him at a rodeo, of all things. He was kind and caring. One look at him, his smile, and I fell in love. I knew he had a ranch and that was his life, in his blood. It wasn't as if he could relocate to the city and find a job with his skill set. Ultimately I couldn't live without him."

"That's so romantic," Erica said.

"My parents and family were professional people and less than thrilled with my decision. But I love him, and love is worth every sacrifice. If you're not willing to do what it takes to be with that person for the rest of your life, it's probably not love. I chose to be a ranch wife and never regretted it." She met Morgan's gaze. "Not once."

"Mama never understood my passion for a career. But I also want very much to be a mother."

"Every mother is a working mother. It's just that some women have jobs outside the home, too." His mother's tone was firm and supportive. "But attitudes have changed, and women have more options and support than ever before."

Erica nodded. "I know they'd like for me to be married with a baby coming because they're concerned about the difficulties of being a single mom."

"They love you, that's all. They just want what's best for you."

"I know that. But—" She hesitated a moment, then waved a hand in front of her face. "I'm sorry to talk about my problems."

"I don't mind listening. But trust me on this. Things will be fine. You wait and see." His mother smiled. "Now I have to go. And so do you two. Go learn something." She stood, grabbed her casserole dish, then let herself out the door.

Morgan was alone with Erica. "You feeling better?"

"Yes, actually." She smiled. "It really was nice talking to someone who understands what I'm dealing with. I've probably said this before, but you're lucky to have her, Morgan."

"I won't argue that. But we have our blind spots, too."

She was staring at the door where his mom had just left. "She sure does love your dad."

"Yeah."

Morgan was well aware that the part of her motivational speech about never regretting her choice had been for his benefit. He thought about the woman he'd proposed to and finding out she was pregnant with another man's baby. Oddly, he realized that he hadn't been that shocked. He felt betrayed and angry about the lie, but he wasn't really hurt. In hindsight, letting her go was the easiest thing he'd ever done. And he never regretted it.

He'd met his fair share of women since then. They were sweet, pretty, bold and sassy. Blondes, brunettes and redheads. Shy, forward, fun and serious. But not a single one of them stuck in his mind or heart when he looked in his rearview mirror.

Not until Erica.

He stared at her now. The tension in her eyes and

around her mouth was gone. She was glowing, and no, that wasn't the sun shining through the window. She got to his heart in a way he'd never been gotten to before. She was becoming awfully important to him, but...

Why did there always have to be a *but*?

She had moved heaven and earth to be a mother, have a baby. He had doubts. Not only whether or not he wanted kids, but also about being a good father. Unless he could be sure about both, he had no business saying anything to Erica about his feelings.

Chapter Eleven

"Mama, thank you so much for taking me shopping."

"You are so welcome, sweetie."

Her mother's suggestion had come out of the blue that morning. The olive branch gave her hope that this was the beginning of better times.

Erica burrowed into the butter-soft leather passenger seat of her mother's luxury SUV. They were finally on their way back to the ranch in the late afternoon. More than once after buying a dress for Denim and Diamonds, Erica had suggested it was time to head home but her mother insisted they browse just one more store—a baby store. How could she resist?

"And the thing is," her mother said, chattering on, "Denim and Diamonds isn't that far off. We had to find you a dress."

"A tent, you mean. Just because it has sequins doesn't make that much material less than a parachute," Erica teased. "Seriously, Mom, it's gorgeous. And I can't believe you whipped out your credit card faster than me."

"I wanted to. So I did."

"And the sleepers you got for the baby are—" Emotion cut off the words. But the tiny outfits were too sweet for words anyway. This surprise shopping spree was her mother's way of mending fences, and Erica was happy that Morgan's mother was right about her coming around. "Thank you again, Mama, for everything."

"You're very welcome. It was fun." Angela drove down the road toward the main house. "I don't know about you, but I can't wait to sit and have a tall glass of iced tea."

"Sounds like heaven."

Her mother parked by the front door and they exited the car. Erica grabbed her dress and the bags of baby things out of the back.

"I'll open the front door for you." Her mother hurried to it, then stood back to let her go in first.

Erica had barely crossed the threshold when she heard, "Surprise!"

"What—" She looked around the entryway decorated with blue and pink balloons that said Baby. Streamers were hanging from the ceiling, and fresh flower arrangements graced the tables. "What is this?"

"A baby shower," her mom said. "Mel's idea."

"My friend Brittany did all the work," Melanie explained. "She's an event planner and very good at it."

Erica looked at her mother. "You knew about this and kept it a secret?"

"Of course. My job was to get you out of the house while everything was being set up." Her mother took the dress and bags from her.

"You played the part perfectly. And I quote, 'just one more store.'" She was completely surprised. "I can't believe this is for me."

"You're the only one here who's pregnant." Mel grinned at her.

Erica glanced at the women gathered there and smiling at her. She recognized Amanda, who was engaged to Morgan's brother Holt.

Deborah Dalton stood beside her. "I love baby showers."

"I'm glad you're here." Erica smiled at her just before her gaze landed on Daphne Taylor, Jordan's sister. "Thank you all for coming."

"Now that our mother-to-be is here, it's my job to make sure everyone has a good time." Mel's friend Brittany was a statuesque woman with light brown skin and beautiful, long dark curls. She wore a form-fitting red dress with a shiny black belt and matching patent leather four-inch heels with a red suede insert. "We haven't officially met yet. I'm Brittany Brandt Dubois, BFF to Amanda and Mel, so I feel as if I know you."

"It's nice to meet you," Erica said. "I never expected to have a shower."

Brittany grinned. "My husband Daniel and I are raising his niece, Hailey. I love her to pieces. She's nine months old and so adorable, but babies are a responsibility. This party is a chance for you to be carefree and have fun before your bundle of joy arrives."

"I don't know what to say. Thank you all." Erica looked ruefully at her outfit, trying not to compare her large sweater, black leggings and cowboy boots to the chicly dressed Brittany. "If I'd known, I'd have dressed up."

"It's not called a surprise for nothing."

She looked up and saw Malone standing at the back of the group. He was the only man there and looked completely fearless. "The food is all set out on the dining room table. So if you ladies will move this party into the other room, I'll start taking drink orders."

There was a rousing sound of agreement, then Mel escorted her to the seat of honor in the great room. Brightly wrapped packages decorated with rattles and pacifiers were stacked around the wing chair.

The women settled on the leather sofa and temporary chairs set up for the occasion.

Brittany took charge in a firm but charming way. They played games and then it was time for food. Malone was on duty to serve.

"We'll have cake soon," Brittany said afterward, "but now it's time for presents."

Erica opened a seemingly endless line of boxes of disposable diapers, baby lotions, tiny sleepers, receiving blankets, a baby monitor, even a thermometer.

She looked around at this incredibly generous group of women who'd come together for her. Even though she'd only known them a short time. "This is so wonderful. I don't know how to thank you all. I'm speechless—"

"Wait. There's one more." Her mother brought over an unwrapped white box and handed it to her.

"What's this?"

"Open it and see."

Erica lifted the lid and pushed aside the protective tissue paper to reveal a small, white dress, delicate lace-covered booties and a stretchy headband with floral appliqués. "Mama? This is gorgeous."

"That was your christening gown. I saved it for you. For your baby."

Erica couldn't count how many times today she'd been overwhelmed, but this was right at the top. She hugged her mom. "Thank you."

"You're welcome." Her mother gently tucked a strand of hair behind her ear and looked at her with love shining in her eyes. "Now, enjoy the rest of your party."

"That's excellent advice because pretty soon it will be all baby, all the time," Amanda said.

"It's a good thing they're cute, adorable and cuddly when they're born," Deborah chimed in. "Because for the first few weeks it's all about changing diapers, trying to interpret the different cries and getting up in the middle of the night to feed them."

"That's true." Her mother sat next to Morgan's mom on the sofa and smiled at the other woman. "You can't even get a smile out of them for the first few weeks. And don't even get me started on teething."

"Oh goodness." Deb rolled her eyes. "The first time Morgan got sick he was about three months old. There's nothing scarier than a sick baby—" She must have seen something in Erica's face because she added, "But babies are incredibly resilient. A little runny nose barely slows them down."

Erica looked at the open packages piled on the floor beside her and fixated on the thermometer. The baby chose that moment to move and stretch. Something, probably a foot, lodged up against her ribs and made her sit up a little straighter.

Suddenly the enormity of the challenge she was facing became all too real. Whatever had possessed her to think it was a good idea to have a baby all by herself? She alone would be responsible for raising this tiny human. Oh dear God…

Somehow she managed to keep the panic at bay through cutting the cake and the random girl talk that followed until the shower was over. She said all the right things, thanked everyone again for coming.

Since Deborah had been dropped off and had to wait for a ride home, she insisted on helping Malone put away leftover food in the kitchen. Amanda and Brittany were pitching in, too. Erica was alone with her mother and just couldn't hold back the anxiety any longer. She burst into tears and almost instantly was wrapped in a familiar, warm embrace.

"What's the matter, sweetie?"

"Oh, Mama, I don't think I can do this."

"I'm pretty sure this is your hormones talking, but let's sit down and you can tell me what's wrong." Her mother led her back to the sofa, where she sat and held her hand. "Now, talk to me."

Erica met her mother's gaze through a blur of tears and was glad she couldn't see the disappointment that was no doubt there. "I'm scared."

"About the birth?" She squeezed the hand still in her own. "You're preparing for that with your class. When the time comes, you'll be ready with all the tools you'll need to make it a positive experience."

Including Morgan, she thought. But after the baby

was born he'd be gone. She looked at the infant thermometer again.

"No, Mama, it's not the birth I'm worried about. It's when I have to take care of a newborn. I'm so afraid I'll do it all wrong and mess this child up. I'm scared that I'll disappoint my baby the way I have you and Daddy."

"Oh, Erica—" Her mother looked astonished. "Is that really what you think?"

"That's how it felt every time I picked my own path instead of yours."

"I didn't realize—" Angela pressed her lips together for a moment. "It never occurred to me that we didn't tell you often enough how proud we are of you. We constantly tell other people how wonderful you are."

"Really?"

She nodded. "We could not be prouder of you. And I can't stress this enough. You are not alone. Your brother and Mel. Your dad and me. Grandpa Alex. Malone. We're all here for you. I'm truly sorry you feel judged. Although, in all fairness, when you came home it was a shock to see you so pregnant when we had no idea about the baby. It was an adjustment and that takes time."

"I'm sorry, Mama. I knew there would be questions about the baby's father, but I should have told you. I just didn't know how."

"Tell us what?"

Erica just had to get this off her chest and hope she had the words to explain in a way that her mother would understand. "Promise me you won't tell Daddy. I know you tell him everything, but you have to swear you won't say anything about this."

There was a wary expression on her mother's face, and she was silent for several moments, obviously conflicted. Finally, and reluctantly, she nodded. "I won't say anything."

"Okay. The thing is, I went to a sperm bank and was inseminated. I've never met the father of this baby, but I have a medical history and a lot of information." Erica took a breath and blew it out. "Daddy's worried about him showing up to try to get something out of us. That will never happen."

"I see. And you felt you couldn't tell us?" Angela asked.

"I was afraid you guys would think I was crazy or foolish, or both. But I felt it was my only choice. My relationship with Peter ended. There was no one in my life and I was pushing thirty. I couldn't help feeling it was now or never, after what you went through…"

"The miscarriages. My bout with depression after."

"Yes."

Her mother sighed and it was a sad sound. "After the miscarriages, my heart broke when the doctor finally told me that I just couldn't carry a baby.

First I felt as if I had done something wrong. Then it felt wrong to not be content with the two beautiful, healthy children I already had. I was only a little older than you are now."

"I was so scared, Mama. I remember that you didn't even want to eat. You weren't sleeping and didn't want to get out of bed. I was afraid you were going to die."

"I'm so sorry you were afraid for me." Angela's eyes teared up. "You brought me peanut butter sandwiches and read to me. You tried so hard to help. I think the only reason I snapped out of it was you, Erica. You made me push myself to put one foot in front of the other."

"You couldn't help it, Mama. And I understand a little better how you felt now that I'm going to be a mother, too."

"And I made you afraid you might never be one." Angela sighed. "That's why you moved heaven and earth to get pregnant."

"Yes." Erica smiled, knowing her mother understood. "But I'm not sure Daddy will get it. Please, don't say anything to him."

"There's something you need to understand, sweetie."

"What?"

"Your father and I want so very much to be grandparents. You know we have for a very long time."

"Yes. You guys aren't subtle." Erica was glad when her mother smiled at that.

"It doesn't matter how this baby came to be, he or she will be loved to the moon and back. Fair warning, though, if you let us be grandparents, I can't promise we won't spoil our grandbaby."

"Oh, Mama—" Erica put a hand over her mouth and nodded. "Yes, please. I would like that very much."

They cried and hugged and laughed. It was cleansing and so very freeing to get all of the hurt out in the open.

"You know—" Her mother brushed a tear from her cheek. "You're going to find out all the joys and challenges of raising a child. And it is joyous."

"I'm glad you'll have my back."

"I absolutely will. In that spirit, here's a piece of motherly advice, just something to tuck away. You may not always understand or approve of your child's choices, but that doesn't mean you won't support and love them unconditionally. Always."

"Like you do me?"

"Yes. And your brother, too." Her mother nodded. "The hardest part is letting go. Standing back without being able to make things better when your children get hurt. In good times and bad, you'll be there for them. No matter what."

"I'll remember that from now on, Mama."

"And one more thing. You took care of me when

you were just a little girl and managed to help me out of that downward spiral. Even then your maternal instincts were working overtime. Never doubt that you're going to be a fantastic mother."

Tears blurred Erica's eyes and she sniffled. "That means so much to me coming from you. Thank you."

It was a relief to finally unburden herself. Her mother would somehow make her father understand there was nothing to worry about from the baby's father. She remembered Morgan had asked if she was in love with the guy. Maybe he was a little jealous?

Wishful thinking. All she knew was that if Morgan hadn't been there for her from the moment they met, she would have been so completely lost. Counting on him had come fast and easy. But she still couldn't decide whether that was a good thing.

Morgan parked his truck outside of Erica's house and waited for his mother. His dad had dropped her off because her car was in the shop and Morgan had volunteered to pick her up when his father got sucked into a spirited game of Go Fish with Robby. Morgan told himself it was about helping out his parents and that was true. But there was another reason. Getting even a glimpse of Erica wouldn't bother him a bit. His mom texted that she'd be a few minutes, so he got out of the truck and leaned against the front of it.

The house lights were on making it almost as bright as day out here. And he focused all his at-

tention on the front door. That's why he didn't see
Gabe Abernathy approaching and wasn't braced for
the usual confrontation.

"Morgan Dalton. Just the man I wanted to see."

"Oh?" He straightened away from the truck.

"What do you want with my sister? Why are you
going out of your way for her? She's having a baby
soon. Most guys would be running away as if her
hair was on fire. You must have an angle. What is
it?"

"You think I'm after something just because my
family doesn't go back generations like yours? Because we bought the land instead of inheriting it?
That doesn't make us bad people."

"You should see someone about that chip on your
shoulder. I never said you were bad people."

"You didn't have to say it." But Morgan wondered
if the guy had a point about him being overly critical.

Gabe shook his head. "My sister has enough to
deal with. She doesn't need some guy taking advantage of her."

"You're dead wrong and way out of line. Erica is
my friend. That's it." Friend fell far short of what he
felt for her, but Morgan didn't understand it completely himself. He wasn't going to try to put it into
words to appease her overprotective brother.

"I don't believe that's all there is to it."

"Not my problem to convince you otherwise."

Morgan shrugged and slid his hands into the pockets of his sheepskin jacket.

Gabe looked more concerned than hostile. "I just don't understand. What do you want with my sister?"

Her. I just want her.

The truth was that he really couldn't blame Gabe for asking. If he had a pregnant sister and some guy who wasn't the father was hanging around her, he would want to know why. On the other hand, what would Gabe say if Morgan confessed that he had feelings for Erica that were more than friendly? He was having trouble wrapping his own head around that.

Just then the front door opened and he saw Amanda and her best friend Brittany. But Morgan only had eyes for Erica, who was walking out with them, looking radiant and happy. His heart seemed to skid sideways in his chest in the most unsettling and extraordinary kind of way.

"Hi, Gabe," Amanda said. "How are you? What are you doing here?"

He smiled and the protective expression disappeared. "I was hoping to catch you. I was wondering if your internet search has turned up anything new on my great-grandfather's daughter."

She shook her head. "I'd have called right away if it had. Without more information, something to go on, I'm stuck. Wish I had better news."

"I'm going to see Gramps again tomorrow," Erica said. "Maybe this time he'll say something to me."

"Would you like me to go with you?" Gabe asked.

Morgan didn't miss the look the other man slid in his direction. As if he'd expected Morgan to offer and beat him to it. The fact was he'd been about to. She told him seeing her grandfather unresponsive wasn't easy, and he wanted to be there for her. He had no idea why, but helping Erica seemed to be hardwired into him.

"Thanks, Gabe," she said. "I'd really appreciate that."

"Of course."

"Mel will be out momentarily. Are you ready to go?" Brittany asked Amanda. "We came together."

"I am. But since Morgan is here I can hitch a ride back with him and Deborah," Amanda answered. "Come to think of it, why are you here? I thought Neal was going to pick her up."

"I volunteered because he and Robby were playing a game, and I wasn't doing anything important."

"Hmm," Erica said wryly, "Could one surmise that you think an adult spending time with a child is important?"

"Yes." Morgan suspected she was trying to make a point, but he wasn't going there. "That and my dad has a cold. Best if he stays in where it's warm."

"Okay, then. I'll ride back with you, Morgan."

Amanda hugged her friends one last time. "I'll get Deborah."

"And I'll go inside with you to get Mel," Gabe said.

"And I'll say good night." Brittany waggled her fingers at everyone and walked to her car.

Suddenly it was just Morgan and Erica. He resisted the urge to say "alone at last."

"So, how was the shower?"

"I was completely surprised," she admitted. "My mom was actually in on it. She even took me shopping and bought some adorable little clothes for the baby. And she gave me my christening outfit. I was just blown away."

"I'm glad it went well." And he got to see her, although he could have skipped the confrontation with her brother.

She must have heard something in his voice because her eyebrows drew together. "What were you and Gabe discussing a few minutes ago? When I walked outside?"

"Just small talk."

"Really? Because I'd swear you were looking at him as if he was a cattle thief and horse rustler all rolled into one."

"I didn't know I was," he hedged.

"Come on, Morgan. This is me. I've gotten to know you pretty well. My brother said something to make you angry. I'm betting it was about me."

So much for bluffing. She was way too smart and observant for that. "He asked me what I wanted from you."

"What did you tell him?"

"That we're friends."

"Hmm." She frowned. "From the look on his face, I'm guessing he didn't buy that."

"Not even a little bit."

She sighed. "Just give it time. He'll come around."

"I won't hold my breath."

"I didn't think my mother would come around either," she said.

"Even though you preached hope and giving people a chance?"

"Even though." Her expression was sheepish. "The thing is, I didn't really believe what I was saying. And I was wrong. Today all the little infant things made me freak out about raising this baby by myself. My mother gave me a great pep talk and I ended up telling her about going to the sperm bank."

"Really?" That surprised him.

She nodded. "She understood why I did it. If she can do that, my brother will eventually understand that you're a good man. You'll see."

He was skeptical. Her brother had already made up his mind that Morgan was using Erica for some underhanded reason. Truthfully Morgan couldn't wrap his own mind around what was going on with him. Why he would do anything for her and couldn't seem to help himself. If he had this under control, he wouldn't have kissed her. That touch of his mouth to hers had opened the dam and he wasn't sure how to stop wanting her.

them hungry, and shall drowsiness amongst the big

Chapter Twelve

It had been a hard day. Erica had gone to see her great-grandfather again and he still didn't know her at all. Feelings of helplessness and disappointment gave way to recurring guilt for having lived far away and not making an effort to see him while he was still responsive. The family dinner that followed with Gabe, Mel and her folks had been a little sad, but the food was fantastic.

Maybe sensing that the Abernathys needed comfort, Malone had outdone himself with a roast and all the trimmings. As they ate, they told stories of Gramps during healthier, happier times that made them laugh. And if all that wasn't enough for big-time comfort, there was cheesecake for dessert.

Now she was sitting beside Gabe at the kitchen table while Malone finished putting away leftovers and washing pots and pans. Mel had excused herself because she had work to do. The folks were watching TV in another room. She and her brother stayed put for some reason. Maybe he felt the need to bond. She sure did.

"Thanks for going with me today." Erica wrapped her hands around the mug of tea Malone had insisted on giving her. "It's hard to see him, but I'm glad I wasn't alone. Having you there made the whole thing so much easier."

He took a sip of his coffee, then smiled. "What kind of a big brother would I be if I didn't support my little sister?"

"Well, it's much appreciated." She reached over and touched his forearm for a moment. "And speaking of the whole big brother thing, you can stand down with Morgan Dalton. He's not a threat to me."

"Do you know that for sure?" Her brother's eyes narrowed. "Have you asked yourself why he's around? Always there for you?"

"Maybe because he's a nice person. What other reason could there be?"

"He wants something."

"What could he possibly want?" She laughed. "I

don't have much money and even if I did, his family is pretty wealthy."

"The rumor is that his father won it gambling."

The rumor was true. "So what does it matter where the money came from? It's not ill-gotten gain. And doesn't change the fact that Morgan is a wealthy man."

"What about the baby?"

"Oh please. My life is a soap opera but not to the point where he'd kidnap my child and sell it to a desperate couple who couldn't have one of their own." She laughed again, and it was a welcome relief from the sad day. "Look, he's a really good guy. Trust me. You'll see."

"I don't know." There was doubt in his voice.

"Seriously, Gabe, it's not about the baby. And—"

"What?" he asked when she stopped.

Erica looked at him. "He's not sure he wants children. So what could he possibly want from me except to be my friend?"

Gabe studied her and a gleam stole into his eyes. "Are you in love with him?"

"Of course not," she said. The response was automatic, but the question made her think.

She liked everything about Morgan, from his sense of humor to his loyalty and friendship. It didn't hurt either that he was awfully good-looking. And she couldn't deny that every time she saw him, her heart just swelled with something wonderful that she refused to name. When she wasn't with him, she longed to be. At the Harvest Festival, when he kissed her, it was the most magical kiss ever.

But was she in love? She sure hoped not. When the baby was born, his promise would be fulfilled. She would be immersed in raising her baby, and he would still be an eligible bachelor. Their relationship would be nothing but a memory, and that made her sad.

Malone finished drying the big pot he'd used for the mashed potatoes and set it on the stove. "More coffee, Gabe?"

"Yes. Thanks, Malone."

"Sure thing." The cook brought over the pot and refilled the mug. "How about you, Erica? More tea?"

"No. Thanks." She smiled at him before he nodded and walked back to scour the roasting pan. She was glad he'd interrupted the conversation because she had no answers for her brother. "Gramps sure didn't say much," she commented, deliberately turning the conversation away from herself.

"I really hoped he would." Gabe shook his head. "You did your best, chattering away about all kinds of things. I was hoping that the two of us there together might jar him out of wherever he is. But he was the same."

"It's hard to picture Gramps as a young man," Erica said. "And to have the responsibility of a baby when he was hardly more than a boy himself."

"Yeah."

"It must have been agonizing for him to give up his baby girl."

Gabe nodded. "He didn't have any family support. In fact just the opposite. Grandpa Alex hardly remembers his grandparents except that they were not the warm and fuzzy type."

"That must have been awful for Gramps. I know you and Mama and Daddy aren't doing the dance of joy about my baby, but no one is pressuring me to give him or her up for adoption."

"We would never do that," he protested.

"Well, I wouldn't—I couldn't give up my child even if there was pressure to. I love this baby so much already. I can't imagine not being there for the first smile, first steps, first word. The thought of it makes me so angry that Gramps was forced to give up his baby girl." Her brother was suddenly staring at her as if she had fire coming out of her eyes. "What?"

"I'm such an idiot."

"Well, I've always suspected as much," she teased. "But what makes you so sure?"

"It just hit me." There was wonder in his expression. "I'm going to be an uncle."

"Really?" she said wryly. "Imagine that. It's what happens when your sister has a baby. You just now figured that out?"

"Of course I knew. I just—" He shrugged. "I just

didn't think about it that way. Too busy resenting you for living so far away. Blowing through on holidays."

"I truly regret that."

"You had your reasons, I guess. And it really doesn't matter now. You're having a baby. Bringing a new life into the world." He looked at her pregnant belly and a warmth stole into his eyes. "I'm going to be an uncle."

"You are."

"I'm going to be the best uncle you've ever seen," Gabe said grinning.

"I know you will because you've always been the best big brother a girl could ask for." She swallowed the lump of emotion in her throat. "I've missed you. Been so busy proving my independence that I didn't realize how much I missed you until I got home. I love you."

"I love you back. And I'm going to love this baby so much. In case you aren't aware, you should prepare for the reality that our parents are going to spoil this kid rotten."

"I'm not so sure. Mama maybe. She's come around. But Daddy—" She shook her head, wishing things could be different.

"Give him time. A boy will be hard enough for him to resist. But a girl? Forget about it." Gabe grinned. "If you have a daughter, she'll wrap him around her little finger."

"You think?"

"I know so. If you have a girl who looks like you, she'll be the prettiest little girl in the world."

"Oh, Gabe—" Her eyes got misty at his compliment.

"What did you say?" Malone shut off the faucet and came over, still holding a saucepan. There was an odd expression on his rugged face.

Gabe gave him a puzzled look. "I said, if Erica has a daughter who looks like her, the baby will be the prettiest little girl in the world."

Erica had forgotten he was there. She'd known this man since she was a kid and had never seen him quite so intense. "Why, Malone? What is it?"

"It just reminded me of something your Gramps said a while back…" There was a strange and thoughtful expression in his eyes, as if he was trying to remember something.

"What did he say?" Gabe prodded.

Malone hesitated for a moment. "It was something like you just said. And I think it was about five years ago. I remember that because it was when his memory was starting to go. A lot of the time he seemed stuck in the past."

"What was it?" Gabe said again.

"I remember him going on and on about 'the prettiest little girl in the world.'" He looked from Erica to Gabe. "And he said a name. It wasn't his wife, Cora. So I thought it might be an old girlfriend."

"Was the name Winona?" Erica asked.

"Nope." Malone shook his head.

"But it was someone from his past." There was excitement in Gabe's voice. "What if he wasn't talking about a woman? What if it was about his daughter? Beatrix?"

Malone thought for a moment. "Nope. That wasn't the name he said."

"Are you sure?" Gabe pushed.

"Yeah." Malone looked apologetic and frustrated with himself. "I just can't recollect what the name was." He tapped his forehead. "It's right there, but I can't grab onto it. I'm sorry, Gabe."

"Don't beat yourself up over it," her brother said. "Sometimes trying too hard just pushes things even more out of reach. It'll come to you."

"Hope so. Sure would like to help find her."

"I know you would."

Although Gabe did his best to hide it, Erica could hear the disappointment in her brother's voice. Like Amanda said, without another clue of some kind, the search for their great-grandfather's daughter was going nowhere. An Abernathy was out there and they all wanted to find her. For just a moment, Malone's comment stirred hope that things would break their way. A name from the past that would unlock a mystery.

Then, just as fast, that hope was gone because there was no way to force a memory. Gramps too had some memories of his lost baby girl buried so deep in his mind they couldn't be reached, and it was frustrating.

Memories were funny and precious and bittersweet. Pretty soon Morgan would be only a memory. When she was as old as Gramps, would she remember him? After she gave birth, the time she spent with him would become the past. That was tearing her apart. She couldn't wait to say hello to her baby, but her heart didn't want to say goodbye to Morgan.

Morgan sat in the passenger seat of his father's old truck. They'd been mending fences at the outermost boundary of Dalton's Grange, and it was a big piece of land. That meant a long ride back with Neal Dalton, the last man on earth he wanted to spend time with. No matter how he grudgingly respected the man's work ethic and his dedication to a physically demanding job, Morgan couldn't forgive the hurt to his mother. And the longer the ride went on, the more awkward the silence became. He was determined not to break it.

But apparently his father had no problem doing it. "Sure is a pretty day. There's nothing like a clear Montana sky. A little cold, though. Winter is coming, so it's a good thing we got this job done while the weather is holding."

Morgan thought about not responding, then changed his mind. But one word was all the man would get. "Yeah."

Neal glanced over, then back to the road in front of him. "Your mom said Erica's baby shower was really nice. She had a good time. Thanks for picking her up."

"No problem." Unless you counted Gabe Abernathy and his suspicious attitude. The guy was way off base. Morgan didn't want anything from her. Not really. Nothing except to spend time with her. Picking up his mom from the baby shower was one way to make that happen.

His father's even-tempered disposition was starting to make Morgan feel like a complete jerk. He could throw the man a bone. "How's your cold? Any better?"

"Yeah. Your mother insisted I take it easy and filled me with liquids and chicken soup. Cold and flu don't stand a chance against her soup. And her, for that matter."

Morgan didn't want to smile but he couldn't help it. "That's Mom."

"Yeah." The man looked over again, just for a moment. "Appreciate you and your brothers picking up the slack for me around the ranch."

"No big deal. Like you said—no one argues with Mom."

After that, neither of them seemed to have anything to say. Morgan just wished this ride would be over.

"How's Erica?" Neal finally said. "Baby's due pretty soon, right?"

"A couple weeks." Morgan smiled to himself just thinking about her. She grumbled about growing big as a house, but he thought she got more beautiful every day.

"She sure is a pretty young woman," his dad said. It was like the man could read minds. "Your mom sure likes her. Said Erica's mom is real nice, too."

"Yeah."

His father waited for more, and when it didn't come he finally said, "Sure is nice of you to support her and be her labor coach. It would be hard to go through that alone."

"I suppose."

"No supposing about it. Bringing a baby into this world is pretty scary." His father maneuvered the truck around a big rut in the unpaved road, then they continued to bounce along. "I remember when your mom was first pregnant. You weren't planned. And I have a confession to make."

"Another one?" Morgan said sarcastically.

Neal ignored that. "I wasn't sure I wanted to be a father. Didn't really know whether I wanted kids."

Wasn't that just great? Morgan took after his unfaithful father. "So why'd you have four more then?"

"Because of you." His dad looked over, then back to the road.

"What about me?"

"You were the first and I worried about everything. Not your mother. She had a knack for knowing when to worry and when to let it go." He laughed and shook his head. "And she loved being pregnant. Was never healthier or more beautiful, but that didn't stop me from being anxious about her. Anything could happen. And she was…"

In spite of himself, Morgan was pulled into this walk down memory lane now. "Mom was what?"

"Everything," Neal said reverently. "She's my whole world and she gave up a successful career and a different kind of life because she loved me. The isolation of ranch life was a lot to ask of her."

"But she did it."

"And I always felt the pressure to give her whatever she wanted so she didn't feel like she made the wrong choice and wasted her life on me."

"And she wanted a baby," Morgan prompted.

"Yeah."

"And you didn't?" he challenged.

"I won't lie. I wasn't fully on board." He suddenly grinned at a memory. "Not until I saw you for the first time." He glanced over, probably to see how Morgan reacted to that statement. "Don't take this the wrong way, but you were not all that good-looking right after you were born. Neither were your brothers. All red and scrunchy. But I had a son. And from that day on the feelings were, are—"

"What?" Morgan asked.

"Bigger than anything I'd ever felt in my life. I loved your mom, but the son we made was—" Hands on the steering wheel, he shrugged. "I can't even describe the love. Maybe as big as this Montana sky."

Morgan looked out the truck window at the blue that seemed to go on forever. That was a lot of love. One of his earliest memories was this man putting him on a horse, patiently teaching him to ride it. Letting Morgan follow him around the ranch. He never raised his voice, even when his brothers came along one by one and the chaos multiplied.

Morgan had a clear memory of resenting Holt for stealing his own time with their father. As the oldest he was expected to share his mother, but he wasn't in the mood to graciously share his father, the man he hero-worshiped.

"If you love mom so much, how could you cheat on her?"

His father pressed his lips together and shook his head slightly. "I messed up big-time. It wasn't a pattern, but happened more than once."

"Slipups," Morgan said angrily.

"Too much liquor was always involved."

"That's just an excuse. The least you can do is be honest and take responsibility."

"Maybe you can't understand, but I have to say this. I was always stressed about money. Ranch operations depended on cash flow. I had doctor bills for my family. The price of beef went up and down. Too much rain or snow could affect the cost of hay, loss of livestock. It was all about keeping the ranch going for you boys and your mom. Sometimes the strain got to be too much. Drink took the edge off."

Morgan remembered several times when his mom had tried to hide that she'd been crying. The man he'd looked up to above all others had broken his mother's heart. Morgan had been hurt and angry the first time. A couple of slipups later and his anger had boiled over.

He'd been the first to leave the family ranch and hire on with another outfit. One by one his brothers all followed him. And for the same reason. They couldn't stand to see their mother with the man who treated her that way.

"Tell me one thing," he snapped.

"Okay." There was no hesitation in his father's voice.

"Why did she forgive you? Why in hell did she take you back?"

"You'll have to ask her that, son. But I thank God every day that she did." Neal let out a long breath. "The money I won to buy this ranch was the second-luckiest thing that ever happened to me."

"What was the first?"

"The day the minister asked your mother if she would honor and cherish me and she said, 'I will.'" He looked over for a moment. "The day I won that money I vowed it would be a new beginning for Deborah and me and our boys. I could finally give the family I love the lifestyle they deserve."

Morgan stared at the man's profile. "You do know that my brothers and I are only here to work the ranch because Mom asked us to, right? That, and we needed to make sure she'd be okay."

"I'm aware." There was sadness and acknowledgment of the fault in his tone. "I know none of you trust me."

"How can we?"

He made the turn onto the road that led to the barn. "I don't expect you to believe this after what I've done, but I love her, too. I'd give my life for hers. I'm going to make it up to her."

"You're right. I don't believe you." He huffed out a breath. "I used to look up to you and you let me down. Tell me why in the name of God I should believe what you're saying now."

"I don't drink anymore, Morgan. Not at all." He glanced over and the resolve in his eyes was unmistakable. "Marriage has its ups and downs, but if a man and woman really love each other, they can work through tough times and make it to the other side. Stronger than before. I swear on everything I hold dear that I only have eyes for your mother. I'm so grateful that she loves me enough to give me another chance. And, son, I hope you and your brothers will follow her lead and do the same."

His father drove up to the barn and parked. "I'm just asking you to keep an open mind."

When he got out of the truck Morgan's mind

wasn't necessarily open but it was sure spinning. As he helped unload the tools, he thought back to the day he'd come to Dalton's Grange. From that day on he couldn't recall seeing his father consume alcohol. Because of his anger and resentment, he'd never noticed before.

He'd never seen his mother happier, and more than once she'd told them this was the best time of her life. Having her sons nearby was such a blessing. And his parents were like newlyweds, always touching, exchanging secret looks, kissing like teenagers when they thought no one was watching. And now this. His dad had come out and asked for another chance.

Morgan remembered Erica saying more than once that they both should give their families an opportunity to patch up relationships. The night of the baby shower, she'd told him she and her mom were on the mend.

It occurred to him that everyone made mistakes, but attempting to right those wrongs was the foundation of character. Maybe Erica was right about second chances.

When the truck bed was empty, Morgan lifted the tailgate and made sure the thing was securely latched. His father stood beside him and their gazes met. There was no mistaking the sincerity in the other man's eyes.

Morgan stuck out his hand. "I believe you, Dad."

Neal's mouth trembled just for a second, and there

was a suspicious moisture in his eyes. Then he shook hands and pulled Morgan in for a hug. "Thank you, son."

Morgan nodded and felt his own throat tighten as a weight lifted from him. Holt seemed at peace with their father, but the rest of his brothers would have to figure out where they stood with him. Morgan wouldn't interfere or influence them one way or the other. But ending hostilities was the right decision for him.

And he had Erica to thank for putting cracks in his attitude in order to give understanding and common sense a way in.

It was a relief to know the man loved being a dad and was a good one. That meant there was hope for Morgan. If—

He pulled up short. For such a small word, *if* had awfully big consequences. Did he want complications? A baby? All he knew for sure was that he couldn't shake the feeling of wanting Erica, and he had no idea what he was going to do about it.

Chapter Thirteen

Erica checked her appearance in the mirror over the bathroom sink and nodded with satisfaction. Her hair was in a ponytail for tonight's childbirth class in which they would be practicing breathing and relaxation techniques. She hadn't seen Morgan since that brief, unsatisfying encounter after her baby shower. There had been barely enough time to say hello, and she wanted more.

She was very aware of the time limit on their involvement and wasn't trying to fight it anymore. Trying to turn off her feelings to avoid emotional messiness was pointless. After the baby was born, she would have Morgan withdrawal and would fall back on her memories, but for now she was going to enjoy the time she had left with him.

After applying lipstick, she headed downstairs and found her mom in the great room reading. It was cozy with a fire crackling, and she had a few minutes to visit before leaving to pick up Morgan. "Hey, Mama. Is that a good book?"

"Yes." She marked her place, then set the book aside. "You're going to class?"

"Pretty soon." It was such a relief to be on good terms again. Up front and honest about her situation. If only she could talk to her dad, too. "I'm picking up Morgan."

Angela nodded. "I invited his mother to join the Bronco Valley Assistance League and she seemed eager to be a part of it. I liked her very much."

"I do, too. And I like Mel, too. I talk to her almost every day. She's becoming the sister I never had. My brother chose wisely."

"I feel the same way. And they're meant to be together, although when they first met there was tension, not all of it the good kind." Her mom smiled. "But they worked it out."

"I'm glad." Erica was so happy for her brother, but also wistful for herself. It was possible that she and Morgan were meant to be together, but her pregnancy made that too big a hurdle.

"You and Morgan seem to get along pretty well.

And you have from the very beginning, I hear." Her mother didn't look upset.

"We definitely clicked," Erica admitted. "As friends. We're not like Mel and Gabe. Not romantic."

"Really?" There was a gleam of speculation in her mother's eyes. "You're sure?"

"Yes. Completely." Because he had doubts about being a father. Her family had doubts about him. "And you don't trust him. Why would you think there's anything serious between us?"

"Because of Deborah Dalton. I got a sense about her that she's a good person who raised her boys to be good men. She and I were talking. She knows her son and I know my daughter." Angela shrugged. "We were just playing 'what if.'"

"You know Morgan had words with Gabe that night," Erica said.

"He's protective. And if I hadn't met Deborah, I might agree with your brother's doubts. She's good people. I'd be really surprised if Morgan isn't, too."

"Well, he's certainly been a good friend to me." She looked at her watch. "I have to go or I'll be late for class."

"Can't have that."

"See you later." She leaned over to kiss her mother's cheek, then straightened and headed for the door.

After driving to Dalton's Grange, she saw Morgan waiting for her outside his house. He walked over to the driver's side of the SUV and she opened the window.

"I know you insisted on picking me up, but at least let me drive from here."

"What? You don't trust me?"

"That's not it at all." He leaned over and rested his arms on the doorframe, his face not far from hers. "It seems to me that my job in all this is to take care of you. Driving you there checks that box."

"Okay." She turned off the engine and stepped out. "I'm not too stubborn to accept a generous offer of assistance."

Especially when the man offering it tugged at her heart in a way no man ever had. Telling him no just might not be possible. She took his outstretched hand and walked to the passenger side of her car. He held the door open for her to get in.

"Thank you," she said.

"Don't mention it." He closed her door and walked around the front of the vehicle, then got in behind the wheel. "And we're off."

Erica had to admit it was nice to sit back and be driven. She could get used to this. As soon as that thought popped into her head, she pushed it away. She couldn't let herself think about getting used to anything with Morgan.

"So, what's new?" he asked.

"You mean since my brother practically took your

head off?" She looked over at him, and the dashboard lights revealed the humor on his face.

"Yeah, since then," he said.

"Well, my mom said she really liked your mom. And I quote, 'she's good people.' And she invited your mother to join the Bronco Valley Assistance League."

"What do you know? It's only been a year. And all it took to be accepted by the old guard was you having a baby." He grinned.

"It's a miracle, all right. Along with the fact that my mother and I are still getting along. And you should know that she doesn't seem to object anymore to you being my coach." In fact, Erica strongly suspected her mother of going in the opposite direction. She'd been doing a little matchmaking tonight. It was a sweet thought but doomed to failure.

"Speaking of getting along…" He glanced over at her for a second. "I had a talk with my dad."

"An actual conversation that consisted of more than yup, nope and livestock feed?"

He laughed. "This will shock you. But we discussed our feelings."

"Gasp." She pressed a hand to her chest in mock surprise. "I thought I felt a ripple in the fabric of the cosmos."

"I know."

Erica listened as he told her about his father taking responsibility for his actions, his vow to make it up to his wife and family and especially his promise to Deborah to love her and make her happy.

"So, you and your dad are really speaking to each other?"

"Thanks to you, yes."

"I don't understand," she said. "I didn't do anything."

"You were the one preaching second chances," he reminded her. "Although I don't think your brother is willing to give me even a first chance."

"Gabe is a good man and normally fair, too." She sighed. "But something about you pushes his buttons."

"Yeah, something. Your brother wants to rip my head off, and I've never even touched you."

Except for that kiss. He hadn't done it again, but every innocent touch—helping her into the car. When their arms brushed or he took her hand—it felt like more. And, right or wrong, she wanted this to be more.

She didn't quite trust her voice not to give away her yearning and didn't talk for several moments. After a deep breath she finally said, "Be patient, Morgan. Gabe will come around. I can see you two becoming good friends."

"That's just crazy talk."

She laughed. "You'll see I'm right about this."

"Agree to disagree," he said. "Change of subject. Did you get lots of good stuff at the shower?"

"I did. All I need now is a crib. And a car seat. Can't bring the baby home from the hospital without one."

"I guess so."

He turned the car into the lot at the Women's Health Center and parked. As they walked to the building, Erica had an almost overwhelming urge to slide her hand into his, but managed to hold back. That's not what a friend would do.

When they reached the conference room, only Carla was there. They were the first ones to arrive.

"Hey, you two." The nurse/educator smiled. "How are you?"

"Good." Erica looked up at Morgan as he nodded.

"Your due date isn't too far away," Carla said. "You both must be getting excited."

"I can't wait to hold this little one." She rested her hands on her belly, then she glanced up and saw the expression on Morgan's face, something that looked a lot like longing. Was it possible that he might not want to say good-bye after she had the baby?

By anyone's measure, what he was doing fell into going above and beyond the call of duty. She'd been drawn to him the first time they met at DJ's Deluxe and the feelings had escalated since then. She'd never met anyone like him and had never felt about a man the way she did about Morgan. Before she could take that thought further the other three couples walked into the room.

"Hi, everyone," Carla said. "We're in the pregnancy home stretch now. I hope you've all been practicing your breathing at home, but let's go over it again. So, if you'll all settle on the floor, we'll get started."

Morgan unrolled the mat and she sat on it with him behind her. She could feel the heat of his body all around her and barely resisted the urge to curl into him. He had her back. He'd always had her back and she loved that he did. Before she could think too much about that, Carla explained what they were doing.

"Okay. First stage of labor. Organizing breath. Take in a deep breath as the contraction starts, then slowly breathe out releasing tension from your head to your toes. Slowly inhale through your nose. Exhale slowly through your mouth. Every time you do this, focus on relaxing a different body part."

Morgan spoke quietly into her ear, reminding her of what the instructor had said. "Okay, now you're in active labor. Keep breathing as slowly as possible, speeding it up as the intensity of the contraction increases."

"Okay."

Moments later he gently rubbed her arms. "You're tensing up. Concentrate on your right leg, relaxing your toes, your foot and ankle, up your calf and thigh."

Erica tried her best to follow his directions but

the feel of his breath on her cheek and the sound of his deep voice in her ear made her feel as if he was actually touching her everywhere. And she wanted that so much.

Carla looked at each of them, nodding enthusiastically. "Okay, you're all doing great. Now transition breathing."

"Okay," Morgan said, "Focus on that picture on the wall. You're having a contraction. Breathe in and out through your mouth, Carla said it should be at a rate of one to ten breaths every five seconds. Every fourth or fifth breath blow out a longer one."

"This is really complicated," she said. "I'm really glad you're here."

"Nowhere else I'd rather be."

Morgan put his big hand at the small of her back and began to gently caress. "Okay. Deep breath."

Erica nodded, even though she wasn't certain she could breathe at all with him touching her. The feel of his warm fingers shorted out her brain and made her want to melt into him. Somehow his deep, steady voice penetrated her mental slide, and she followed his instructions.

"Doing great," he said.

His breath was warm on her cheek and her breathing escalated, but not in any kind of controlled way.

"Good job, everyone." Carla smiled at the group. "You're all here to prepare for a positive birth experience. Relaxation is important. If you tense up, discomfort is magnified. Dads, this is where you can step in. If you feel her tensing, give her a big bear hug."

Without hesitation, Morgan wrapped his muscular arms around her and squeezed gently. The embrace was sure and strong and made her feel so safe she could have stayed there forever. His lips were so near her cheek and she felt him hesitate, as if he was going to kiss her but he didn't. Then Carla started giving them more pointers.

As instructed, Morgan gently stroked her forehead, jaw and hands. Rhythmically, he kneaded her shoulders and neck, and she thought she'd died and gone to heaven. He used firm pressure with the palm of his hand to rub her from shoulder to hip, then from thigh to knee.

Erica was fairly certain nothing she'd ever experienced had felt quite so perfect as Morgan's touch. And she didn't think there was a breathing technique in the world that could control her reaction to the exquisite sensation of his hands on her body.

She glanced up at his face and recognized the intensity that turned his eyes a darker shade of blue than normal. At first she thought it was only concentration. Then she saw the pulse throbbing in his neck and knew. He was feeling something for her, too, and it was more than just being her support partner. It was the scariest, most exciting feeling she'd ever had. But where did they go from here?

* * *

Holy crap! Morgan couldn't believe how close he'd come to kissing Erica in that class. Her skin was so soft and she was so beautiful. Time after time, he caught himself and stopped, but there was something in her eyes. Something he'd never seen before. But he couldn't identify it, and she didn't help. She hadn't said a word since he started driving them back to Dalton's Grange.

It was time to break the silence. "Do you want to stop for something to eat? Are you hungry?"

"No, thanks." Her voice was soft and the tone a little unsure, as if she had something on her mind.

"Okay."

He was thinking hard about what to say but could only come up with an apology for wanting her. But he wasn't really sorry at all. God help him.

She was pregnant and he most likely was crazy. But she was the most beautiful, sexiest woman he'd ever met. And if he was being honest with himself, it was more than that. She was sweet, caring, friendly, kind and funny. He'd never met a woman who had it all. Not until Erica.

And now he'd made it weird.

He turned onto the road where Dalton land started, and Erica still hadn't said anything besides no thanks. If he didn't fix this, she was going to let him off, then drive home, and there would be this unspoken, awkward thing between them.

He pulled up in front of his house, but didn't turn off the car's ignition. "You're awfully quiet. Everything okay?"

"Yes—" She sighed. "No."

"I knew it." He shook his head. "It's me, isn't it? I did something—"

"Morgan, no." She released her seat belt and put her hand on his arm. "It's me. I—"

"What?" he asked when she hesitated.

"I haven't been practicing my breathing, and tonight I guess Carla really got through to me how important it will be."

"So, we'll practice," he said.

He nodded toward his house with the light shining in the front window. "In fact, why not now while the class is still fresh in our minds?"

"Really? Are you sure? I know you get up early—"

"It's fine." He put his hand over hers and tried not to notice the heat that shot through him. "I can see that you're stressed about this. That's not good. The best way to deal with it is to practice. What do you say?"

"Okay."

Morgan turned the key and shut off the car. He got out and went around to open Erica's door, then offered his hand to help her out. When her fingers touched his palm, his whole body went tight with need, and fire licked through him. The heat threatened to consume him.

Get a grip, Dalton. Don't be a jerk.

They walked into the house and she looked around. "This is awfully tidy for a single guy."

"If you don't look in the kitchen, my halo will stay all shiny and bright." Teasing cut the tension and that was a relief. "Can I get you anything? Water? Iced tea? Beer?" He held up a hand. "Just kidding."

"I knew that. Water would be great."

"Coming right up." But he was having a beer. It might take the edge off his wanting her more than his next breath. That thought was ironic considering they were here to practice breathing.

On his way to the kitchen he said over his shoulder, "Make yourself comfortable."

"I guess we should sit on the floor like we do in class," she called back.

"Whatever you want."

Morgan grabbed the drinks, brought them into the living room and set them on a table beside the leather sofa. Erica was sitting on the floor.

She glanced over her shoulder and smiled. "Whenever you're ready."

He was so ready. And, damn it, why couldn't he stop thinking in double entendres? *Focus*, he ordered himself. It would be hard to do that since he had to sit behind her. So close. Touching her. Breathing in the scent of her. But this wasn't about him. For her, he would be the best coach on the planet or die trying.

He assumed his position and couldn't help thinking for the hundredth time how good she smelled. How soft and delicate and graceful her neck looked. How much he wanted to see for himself if her skin tasted as sexy as he thought it would.

"Okay—" He braced himself. "Organizing breath. Slow and deep as the contraction starts, then let it out, releasing all the tension from your shoulders, legs and all the way to your toes."

She did as instructed, but he could feel that she wasn't responding to the technique. He wasn't sure what to do except continue instructing and counting. So, that's what they did and went through all the different stages of breathing.

"Do you want to start over again?" he asked.

"No." She said that a little too quickly. Oddly enough, after all that breathing she'd just done, there was a sexy, breathless quality to her voice. "That went okay. I think we work pretty well together."

"Yes, we do." And he could really get used to the nearness of her. The warmth of her burrowing deep inside him, thawing out a place that had been frozen for a long time.

She glanced over her shoulder and said, "How can I ever thank you?"

"By not hating me for how much I still want to kiss you." Morgan wasn't sure he'd actually said that out loud.

Her eyes widened and she blinked up at him. A

couple of seconds passed before she said, "Does that mean you wanted to kiss me before now?"

There was no way to dodge this, so he didn't try. "In class tonight. So many times I came very close to kissing you. It's official. I'm a jerk. I know it. Right there in front of everyone I wanted to just—"

"I wasn't completely sure I didn't imagine that." She turned around to face him and smiled softly. "There's no one here now except you and me."

"What?"

"If you're a jerk, then so am I. It was so hard to concentrate when all I could think about was you touching me and how good it felt." Definitely that was a breathless whisper.

"Erica—"

Morgan saw that his hand was shaking a little as he traced the curve of her cheek with one finger, then kissed where he'd touched. Her eyes closed, and she shuddered just before the sound of her throaty moan burned through him. She leaned toward him, and this time he didn't hesitate, but took her mouth with his own. The touch sparked a bone-melting fire that spread through his blood.

Not here, he thought. Not on the floor.

Without a word, he stood and held out his hand, helping her to her feet before leading her to his bedroom. Both of them were breathing hard when they sat side by side on the bed.

He kissed her again and let his mouth wander over

her cheekbones, her eyes, her chin. He nuzzled her ear and nipped her neck. Settling his hand on her thigh, he moaned with satisfaction as he remembered how badly he'd been wanting to do this.

He slid his fingers underneath her sweater, over her soft skin and found her breast, cupping it in his palm. She was perfect, the most beautiful, most sensuous woman he'd ever held in his arms. He brushed his thumb over the tip and heard her gasp of pleasure.

She leaned her head against his shoulder. "Oh, Morgan. That feels so good."

"I want you, Erica."

"Yes, please," she whispered.

Mindless with desire, he wanted to touch her everywhere and slid his hand over her belly. There was a rippling movement beneath his palm and he froze. As he hesitated, he felt it again, a rolling motion across her abdomen. If ever there was a cold shower moment, this was it. He pulled his hand away as if he'd touched a hot coal. And maybe he had.

Erica was having a baby. That made her a package deal and sleeping with her was not a step to be taken lightly.

"Morgan?" She was frowning at him.

"I felt the baby move."

"I know." She stared at him and not in a good way. "What's wrong?"

In her eyes he saw the exact moment when she shut down emotionally. "It's not what you think."

"And what do I think?" She slid sideways, a bruised look on her face.

"It's just—" He dragged his fingers through his hair, searching for the words to explain. "I don't want you to think I—"

"I don't think anything except—" She stood up and headed for the door. "I need to go."

"Erica, wait. Let me explain."

She'd stopped in the living room and was looking around. "Where did you put my keys?"

"Just wait a damn minute. We need to talk about this," he said.

"There's nothing to talk about. You've made your feelings crystal clear. So it's better to stop this before either one of us gets hurt." She picked up her purse and looked around the room, anywhere but at him. "I'll go."

Morgan wasn't so sure they weren't already in territory where one of them could get hurt. And, for crying out loud, he needed to take fifteen seconds to process everything. She was bringing a life into the world and that was huge. If he was going to be a part of that, he needed to be sure. He never wanted her to think he'd used her.

He'd thought they had a special connection. Was this just an overreaction to his hesitation? Or something else? Maybe he really was just a friend. A rebound guy from Peter and she was still in love with her ex.

"I need my keys, Morgan."

Damn it, were those tears in her eyes? He didn't think he could take it if she cried. Then he remembered he'd put her keys in his jeans pocket and fished them out. He dropped them into the hand she was holding out and managed to do it without touching her.

She walked to the door and opened it. "Good night, Morgan."

"Erica?"

She brushed a hand across her cheek before looking at him. "What?"

"I'm sorry."

She nodded and without another word walked out the door.

Morgan really felt like putting his fist through a wall. Before she came inside things were weird, but he could have worked with that. If he'd just kept his hands to himself, everything would have been fine, but he hadn't. Now he didn't think there was any coming back from this.

Chapter Fourteen

Erica was hurt and disappointed, but she couldn't be mad at Morgan, and that was super annoying. From the beginning he'd been honest about his doubts, but she'd fallen in love with him anyway. *Love.* Four letters italicized. Capital *L.* In a very short time she'd realized he was a forever-after kind of guy and he cared about her, too. She could tell in everything he did. Especially his kisses. She'd hoped he would change his mind about having kids. Being a father. Being a father to her kid. But last night hope died.

When he felt her baby move, the look on his face had told her everything she needed to know. The man wanted no part in her child's life. That meant Morgan could have no part in hers either.

The tears started again and she was exasperated with herself. She couldn't believe that, after crying most of the night, there could still be any left.

Unable to sleep, she'd gotten up early this morning and showered. Did her hair and put on a little makeup. It was her plan to act as if nothing was wrong. Her family had warned her about Morgan. Her mother, father and Gabe had been afraid he wanted something from her. Ha! It was just the opposite. He wanted nothing to do with her. Only Mel had worried about her getting hurt.

And hurt she was. When she and Peter broke up, she'd been frustrated that her plans for marriage and family had fallen apart. In the end, though, the split felt right. With Morgan there was an ache, an emptiness and a feeling that no other man could ever fill up her heart the way he did.

A tear trickled down her cheek, and impatiently she brushed it away. "Oh, for crying out loud…" Not funny.

She slid off the bed she'd made before the sun came up. If she sat there much longer, she was in real danger of dehydrating. Sooner or later she was going to have to go downstairs and put on a brave face for everyone. Best get it over with.

She took one more look in the mirror and winced at her reflection—the red, puffy eyes. Probably there wasn't enough concealer in the world to hide the evidence of her broken heart, but she applied it anyway. Maybe no one would notice. And it was always possible no one would be there.

Apparently luck abandoned her, because only her father and Malone were missing. Her mother and Gabe were sitting at the kitchen table having coffee. The smell of cooked sausage and eggs filled the air. Not even that made her hungry.

Since her brother was here, that probably meant Mel was out of town for work. Gabe did a double take when he saw her. "You look terrible."

"Thank you." She glared at him, then poured herself half a cup of coffee and sat down at the table.

"Aren't you going to have some breakfast? Malone fixed a plate for you and is keeping it warm in the oven," her mother said.

"I'm not hungry."

"You have to eat something, sweetie. Think about the baby."

Everything she did was for this baby. After making the decision to use a sperm bank, she'd reconciled herself to doing the parent thing alone. But that was before Morgan. Couldn't she feel just a little sorry for herself that things hadn't worked out?

"I don't feel like eating breakfast, Mama. I think the baby will be just fine."

Gabe's eyebrows rose as he sipped his coffee. "Someone is grumpy this morning."

"I'm not," she said, "But keep it up and I'm happy to show you just what grumpy looks like."

"I had cravings when I was pregnant," her mother said. "With Gabe it was candy and chips. Junk."

Erica gave him a smirk. "You are what Mama ate."

Their mother held up a hand to cut off his retort. "He's fine, in spite of what I ate. And with you," she said to Erica, "I wanted avocados and fresh melon."

"Nothing sounds good."

"How was your childbirth class last night?" Her mother met her gaze over the mug of coffee as she took a sip.

"It was good. Lots of information." Afterward sucked. Well, not the kissing Morgan part. That was pretty perfect. So was the touching. Right up until the baby moved.

"I'm surprised the guy hasn't backed out of this labor coach thing yet."

Erica slowly looked up at her brother as the reality hit her. She'd been so caught up in Morgan pulling away when the baby moved, she'd forgotten about everything else. After the way she left his house last night, she wasn't sure if he'd back out. Why wouldn't he? And then what would she do for a coach?

Gabe's expression went from easygoing to concerned as he studied her. "Is something wrong?"

"I don't want to talk about it."

"What happened?" her brother demanded. "Did he come on to you?"

If only.

She tamped down that reaction and speared her brother with a hard look. "He's a good man, and someday you're going to realize that. I predict that you two will be good friends."

Her brother snorted. "Fat chance."

"Ask anyone about him. You won't hear a bad word."

"Uh-huh." Gabe shook his head.

"I don't even know what to say to you right now. If I was ten, I'd call you a butthead. And Mama would scold me and tell me not to call you names."

"Okay, then. That's my cue." He pushed back his chair and stood. "You're crabby. That's not calling her names, Mama. It's an adjective. And I have to go."

"Have a good day, Gabe." Angela smiled at him as he walked out the door, then looked at Erica. "Your brother is right. You are in a mood. What's going on?"

"I'm pregnant, Mama." *And the man I love can't handle it. That's what's wrong.*

"You know, honey, it's completely natural for a pregnant woman to feel uncomfortable. Your body is supporting life. Your ankles are retaining enough water to float a cruise ship. Sleeping is hard because there's no comfortable position and bedtime is usually when your little unborn angel decides to do the backstroke."

Erica couldn't help smiling at the exaggerated but all too accurate description. "And your point is?"

"It's no secret we haven't been as supportive of your pregnancy as we could have been. I wonder if you feel that if you complain about being uncomfortable, we'll think you regret your decision. Or that we'll think this is what you get for making your choice. We don't."

"But, Mama—"

Her mother held up a hand to stop her words. "I'm not finished." She took a deep breath. "It also doesn't mean that we'll think you don't love your baby. Or that we won't love your baby. This is our first grandchild."

A tear rolled down Erica's cheek. "Damn hormones."

"I remember it well." A smile teased Angela's lips.

"The thing is, Mama, I know you understand. But you're a mother. I'm afraid Daddy will never be able to forgive me for doing the motherhood thing the way I have."

"Don't sell your father short. He understands more than you give him credit for."

"But more than once I've heard him criticize technology, newfangled contraptions. If it wasn't for science and a little bit of a miracle, I wouldn't be having a baby. Women do it all the time and that choice is widely accepted. But I don't know if he can get over his daughter taking that path."

Her mother didn't respond to that for several moments. She looked thoughtful, then seemed to come to a decision and stood. "Come with me."

"What? Where?" Erica questioned, but stood anyway.

"There's something you need to see. Get your jacket. It's cold outside."

Erica grabbed her poncho from the hook by the back door, then put it on and followed her mother outside. "Where are we going?"

"To the barn."

"Why?"

"Because one picture is worth a thousand words." That cryptic statement was all she would say.

They walked to the ranch outbuildings and into the barn. Erica kept pace with her mother past the hay-filled stalls and to the tack room in a far corner of the structure where her father was working. He was down on one knee and his back was to them as he dragged a paintbrush across something. The smell of wood sealer was faint in the air.

"George," her mother said. "I think it's time you show Erica what you're doing."

He stood and turned toward them. "Angela, it's supposed to be a surprise. I asked you to keep her away while I finish this."

"What's going on, Daddy? What are you doing?"

She moved closer until she was standing right beside him. When she saw it, her heart melted and she pressed a hand to her chest. "Oh my gosh. You made a cradle."

"Yeah." He set the brush on the open can beside him, then looked at her. His gaze narrowed and concern replaced his tender expression. "Are you all right? Is there something wrong with the baby?"

She laughed, although the sound came out a little like a sob, what with hormones and emotions clogging her throat. "I'm fine. So is the baby. Gabe told me flat out that I look terrible. I guess it's unanimous."

"I didn't say that," her father protested.

She moved closer to the sweet little bed suspended between two supports that allowed it to rock. "I can't believe you made this. It's completely wonderful."

She recognized the grain of the wood as what she'd picked up for him that day she'd run into Morgan at the building supply store. Her father had planned this very soon after he'd learned she was pregnant.

She burst into tears and covered her face with her hands. A moment later she felt strong arms come around her.

"Don't cry, honey. Your mama told me about how the baby came to be," he said gently.

"I guess I knew she couldn't keep a secret from you," she blubbered.

"No," he confirmed. "And I don't keep things from her. It's just how we are."

"It's a good way." She looked up at him. "Please try to understand why I had to have a baby this way, Daddy. I know it's not what you pictured for me, but in time I hope you'll be okay with my decision and with me."

"What?" He took her arms and held her away as he stared at her. There was shock on his face as he met her gaze. "How could you even think that? You're my daughter. My flesh and blood. And your child is, too. I love you. Nothing can change that. And I will love him—"

"Or her." His wife smiled at him.

"Right." He grinned. "I'm looking forward to holding this child. Being a grandfather. Don't you ever doubt that for a second."

"I won't. And thank you. For the cradle, too. I love it. And I love you."

She was sad that Morgan would never see this sweet little bed. When she put the baby down to sleep, she would remember her own father's love and be sorry that Morgan would never know what a good father he'd be. She would think of him and regret that he wasn't with her when they could have made a family together, something real and satisfying and wonderful.

Then she looked at her own amazing father and her mother. "Because of how I chose to conceive my child, there's no father in the picture. But he or she will have you guys. And Uncle Gabe and Aunt Mel. We're family. The baby will always be a part of my life and yours. Not like Gramps's daughter. I can't even imagine how he felt not just without support, but pressured to give his child away. This baby is loved and wanted."

Erica held out her arms and drew her mother and father into a group hug. She really did have so much to be grateful for and felt selfish for wishing she could have Morgan, too.

Erica had spent the morning with her brother and the two of them went to see Gramps. It was becoming their habit to go together. And her secret was out. The whole family knew how the baby had been conceived and assured her of their support. That was a great weight lifted from her. She needed that, because what happened with Morgan still hurt a lot.

He kept calling her cell, but she let it go to voice mail. She didn't think there was anything left to say. She would never forget the expression on his face when the baby moved, and it made her sad. The outing this morning helped a little to take her mind off what might have been.

She'd had lunch with her brother, and now she was taking her afternoon walk. Exercise was important, even near the end of her pregnancy when all she wanted to do was sit and feel like a slug. Gabe insisted on keeping her company, and now they were moving past the barn, heading for the corral and the path beyond it.

"How did you think Gramps was today?" she asked.

"Seemed about the same to me. Why?" He slid his hands into the pockets of his down vest.

"I don't know. It just seemed like there was a spark of something in his eyes. And when I put his hand on my belly and the baby moved, I think he might have smiled."

Gabe's expression was sad as he shook his head. "That's just wishful thinking, Erica. It would be great if he was still in there somewhere, but I'm not hopeful."

"Maybe if we could find his daughter..."

"To do that we need a break. Some piece of information that would send us in the right direction." He met her gaze for a moment. "If Malone could just remember the name Gramps said when he was talking about the prettiest little girl in the world..."

"I know," she agreed. "It's human nature to gloss over things. If we knew how important a piece of information would be later, we'd pay more attention."

"Yeah." They strolled along the white fence where a couple of the horses were hanging around. "I've been meaning to ask. Have you heard anything from your attorney about the Barron Enterprises lawsuit?"

"She called the other day to let me know she'd

heard from their legal department. They received the paperwork and were reviewing it. She warned me again that the process could drag on indefinitely. So, I'm glad Jordan Taylor is going to give me a job."

"Hmm."

Erica glanced up at him. "What?"

"He doesn't exactly have a reputation as a guy with a soft heart."

"I've been gone for a lot of years so I don't know much about him lately. But he's always been straight with me."

"Okay." Gabe's tone had a healthy dose of skepticism. "Then I hope he keeps his word and hires you."

"I've already filled out the employee paperwork. And I have a tentative start date." Before she could say more, her cell phone vibrated in her pocket. She fished it out and looked at the caller ID. Speaking of the devil, she thought, and she didn't mean Jordan. She stopped walking and said to her brother, "I have to take this." When Gabe nodded, she hit the green Accept button on the screen. "Peter. Why are you calling me?"

"How are you, Erica?"

The familiar deep voice used to be one that made her happy when she heard it. Not now. "I'm fine. What do you want? My attorney advised me not to speak to anyone from Barron."

"I'm just asking for a few minutes of your time," he said.

Erica noted that her brother's frown deepened. He shook his head slightly but she was curious enough not to hang up. "Okay."

"First of all I want to apologize for my father. He's not used to employees pushing back, and he lost his temper. Firing you was a knee-jerk reaction."

"Your father is a jackass." She saw Gabe grin and give her a thumb-up. "Feel free to tell him I said that."

"He has his moments." Peter cleared his throat. "The thing is, when someone's employment is terminated, there's a procedure and legal is involved. He didn't consult with the company attorneys when he took that action with you."

"So, you're saying that I have grounds for a lawsuit? Since pregnant women are part of a protected class." She wasn't really asking.

And Peter didn't directly respond to the question. "Barron Enterprises is putting together a generous severance package for you."

"A severance package," she repeated for Gabe's benefit. His eyes widened.

"Yes. I would consider it a favor if you would seriously contemplate accepting it."

"And dropping the lawsuit would be a condition." Again she wasn't asking.

"I won't deny that we would like to avoid any negative publicity." That was his lawyer voice.

"I'm sure you would." That was her "you're not going to push me around" voice.

"It's not just that, Erica." There was a sigh on the other end of the line. "I personally want to make sure you're taken care of."

"Really?" The sarcasm in that single word was laced with a good deal of anger. "Funny how it took filing a lawsuit to bring out your sensitive and caring side."

"You're not going to make this easy, are you?"

"Is there some reason I should?"

If he responded, she didn't hear, what with the blood pounding in her ears. She was shaking with anger. No matter how much she told herself it wasn't good for the baby, she couldn't suppress the feeling. In his father's office that day, her life had been thrown into chaos.

It was all about this man's new, pregnant wife, who didn't want to see Erica every day and be reminded that she'd dated her husband first. No one seemed to care that Erica was pregnant, too. She'd had a viable plan and it would have worked. But his father's power trip put her in a position of extreme stress wondering how she was going to support not just herself, but the baby she was carrying.

Finally she calmed down enough to say, "There's no way in hell I'm going to make this easy for you."

"Okay. We deserve that." There was silence for a moment. "Erica, I don't expect you to believe this, but I'm sorry things didn't work out between the two of us. That's my fault," he added quickly. "But I do care about you. And I truly do want to make sure you're going to be okay."

"You're right, Peter. I don't believe you."

"Erica, please—"

"Send the severance package to my attorney. You have her contact information."

"Seriously, Erica, I'm sincerely sorry about everything. It would mean a lot to me if you'd accept my apology."

There was a retort on the tip of her tongue, but she held it back. It occurred to her that she didn't care about this man. In fact, marrying him would have been a very big mistake. She should, in fact, be grateful to him for breaking things off. For being honest about not wanting children, although that turned out to be a lie, since he was expecting with the new wife. So, he just didn't want children with her. But feeling gratitude for his actions was a work in progress.

What she realized was that being angry over her termination was about fairness in business and a yearning for justice. But being angry on a personal level would mean she still had feelings for Peter, and that just wasn't the case.

This was a time for neutrality and generosity of spirit. "I accept your apology, Peter."

"Thank you. And I'll contact your attorney as soon as we hang up."

"Okay. Goodbye, Peter." She ended the call.

She looked at Gabe, who was grinning from ear to ear. "I guess you got the general picture of what's going on."

"The Barrons blinked. They want to pay you off. If you go to court, they're going to take a beating financially and in the media."

"That's the way I see it, too," she said.

Gabe hugged her. "You did great, sis. Way to keep your cool and tell him to go to hell, without actually saying it. Class act."

"Thank you."

She should have felt triumphant as her brother obviously did. But in reality, she felt deflated. Because there was only one person she wanted to share the news with. And she'd walked away from him. Ever since that night with Morgan she'd been wondering if she should have stayed to hear him out. Now it was too late.

That thought made her burst into tears. She looked helplessly at her brother. "I'm sorry. Hormones."

"Is it?" Gabe gave her a challenging look. "You've been in a mood. Ever since the last time you saw Morgan."

"How do you know?" Before he could answer she said, "Mom."

"Something happened with him."

"I don't want to discuss it."

"I don't need a blow-by-blow," Gabe said. "But there's something I do know."

"What?"

"You care about him. And he cares about you. Before you ask how I know that, it's obvious. Why else would he volunteer to be your labor coach?" Gabe shrugged as if it was a no-brainer. "I could see it that first night you met him at DJ's Deluxe. It's why I got so ticked off. You had stars in your eyes, and he had that look a guy gets when he's met a special woman. I don't know him so I didn't like it."

"Really?" She brushed the moisture from her cheeks. "But it wasn't—"

"Don't try to rationalize. It's a big brother thing. Plus, I wasn't subtle," he admitted. "But I *was* wrong. You two care about each other, and you need to talk to him."

That startled her. "Who are you and what have you done with my brother?"

"I deserve that." He looked sheepish. "Shouldn't a person be allowed to change his mind?"

"Of course. I'm just wondering what changed yours."

"I talked to Morgan after the baby shower. I'm a pretty good judge of people and I believed him, that he cares about you," he said. "And I trust your judgment." He leaned over and kissed her forehead. "You know your own mind and you're smart. I love you, sis. And I just want you to be happy."

"Okay—" Emotion choked off her words.

He pointed at her. "Don't you dare cry. It drives guys crazy because we can't fix it. So, just stop."

"I love you, too. And I'll try—" Who was she trying to kid? There was no way that was going to happen. She burst into tears again, and he pulled her in for a hug.

"It's okay. Just talk to Morgan. Do as your big brother says, and everything will be all right."

She wanted to believe that. The problem was, she didn't think Morgan would give her another chance. And she couldn't blame him.

Chapter Fifteen

Morgan glanced into the office in the big house where Neal Dalton was sitting at his desk, scrutinizing the ranch spreadsheets on his computer.

The door was open but he knocked on it and said, "Dad, can I talk to you?"

His father looked up, then removed his reading glasses and set them down on some file folders. "Have a seat."

Morgan closed the door, then walked over and sat in one of the chairs. After taking a big breath he said, "I screwed up with Erica."

"And you're here because out of everyone you know I've had the most experience screwing up?"

"Look, I'm not here to bust you about that—"

"It was a joke. Guess I'll have to work on my delivery." The man sighed. "What did you do?"

Morgan told him about kissing Erica. "Everything was fine and then I felt the baby move. It was awesome, Dad. But it hit me. There's a real baby in there. That sounds so dumb, but it's the honest to God truth."

"I get it. Believe me."

"That changed everything. It wasn't just about the two of us. There's another life involved, and I needed to take that into consideration before moving forward, before, you know—"

"Yeah. So what did you do then?" his dad asked. "After you felt the baby?"

"Nothing. I froze."

Neal looked puzzled. "I'm not seeing the problem, son."

"Erica jumped to a conclusion. She took my reaction to mean that I didn't want her because of the baby. But I just needed a minute to process." He met his father's gaze. "She walked out without giving me a chance to explain why I was hesitating."

"Okay." The other man nodded thoughtfully. "I don't think this is a screw-up. More a misunderstanding. When did it happen?"

"A couple of days ago. I've tried calling her, but it goes straight to voice mail." He lifted his hands, a gesture of pure frustration. "I don't know what to do."

"You have two choices, son. You can let her go—"

"No," Morgan said firmly. That response came straight from the gut, by way of his heart. "That's not an option."

"You're sure?" His dad studied him. "You haven't known her very long."

"I'm absolutely sure. Don't ask me why—"

"Never crossed my mind," the other man said. "With your mom I knew pretty much from the moment I met her that she was the one. Holt proposed to Amanda pretty fast. It might take us Dalton men a while to find the right woman, but when we do, we move to seal the deal right away. But—"

"What?" Morgan asked sharply.

"That means you'll be a father right away. I know that gave you pause not so long ago. And you're right. It's not just you and her to consider. There's another life involved. If you can't accept that fully, best back off now. Otherwise there's a lot of heartache down the road."

"I hear you, Dad. I can't let her go." He shrugged as if to say he just knew. "So, how do I get her back?"

"You need to find a way to show her you're all in. For her *and* the baby. A big gesture. When you figure that out, you drive over there and show her you really mean it."

A gesture. All in for her and the baby. Morgan's

mind was racing, then suddenly he had an idea and it was perfect.

He met his father's gaze, then stood and headed for the door. "Can you spare me for the rest of the day? I've got some stuff to do."

"Of course. And Morgan?"

He stopped with his hand on the doorknob and turned to look at his father. "Yeah?"

"Good luck. If there's anything else I can do, you only have to ask."

"No offense, Dad, but I hope I won't need you." Morgan smiled. If there was one positive thing to come out of this, it was getting back a relationship with his father. "Thanks, Dad."

After the talk, Morgan jumped in his truck and headed downtown. He needed to purchase two things, and the first one was easy, what with just buying the highest consumer rated and most expensive one on the market. The second item took longer. Part of the reason was him calling Erica's cell every half hour to let her know he was picking her up for childbirth class later. And every half hour he got her voice mail. His guts were in a knot, and the uncertainty was killing him.

It was early, but he couldn't wait any longer to see her. He drove to the Ambling A and went up to the brightly lighted porch. He rang the bell, then nervously waited for someone to answer.

When the door was opened, he was surprised to

see Gabe Abernathy. In his mind he'd been running possible speeches to Erica and was unprepared to see anyone else. "What are you doing here?"

"The better question is why are *you* here?"

"I came to pick up Erica." Morgan braced for hostilities. He planned to stand his ground even though he knew the Abernathys didn't trust him. They were just going to have to suck it up and get used to him being around. Oddly enough, her brother didn't look hostile.

"Did she know you were coming to get her?" Gabe's amusement disappeared.

"We have class tonight. And I left messages that I'd be here." Morgan glanced down for a moment. "Would you please let her know?"

"I would be happy to except she left already."

The words felt like a punch to the gut, and Morgan hadn't braced himself for that. "Where did she go?"

"I heard her tell my mom that she was going to her class. Doesn't she usually pick you up?"

"Yeah." But that was before.

"Maybe there's a miscommunication and she thought you were meeting her at the class."

"No. But we will be meeting." Morgan touched his fingers to the brim of his Stetson. "Thanks, Gabe. Sorry to bother you."

"No problem. And, Morgan?"

He stopped and looked over his shoulder. "Yeah?"

"For what it's worth, I'm rooting for you, Coach."

"Thanks."

Morgan wouldn't have thought anything could make him smile, but that did. It helped knowing her brother was on his side, and right this minute he was in no mood to question what had happened to make him change his mind. His focus was on making his case to the person who mattered most to him.

He drove the now familiar route to the Women's Health Center and realized this was the first time he'd come alone. He didn't much like that and hoped it wasn't a bad omen for the rest of his life. When he arrived at his destination, he went up and down the rows of cars until he found Erica's. For a desperate man in need of some hope, he took the empty space beside her SUV as a good sign.

He exited his vehicle, then opened the rear passenger door of his truck, removed the brand-new infant car seat and headed for the building's lobby and the elevator.

His heart was racing as he walked down the carpeted hallway and into the conference room. Carla was there at the lectern. The other three expectant couples sat at the U-shaped tables. When he walked in, all conversation ceased and everyone stared at him. He only had eyes for Erica.

He walked over to her. "Hi. I'd have been here sooner but I stopped at your place to pick you up. Gabe said you'd already left."

Eyes wide as saucers, she nodded. "I didn't think you wanted to do this with me anymore."

"You thought wrong." He set the carrier on the table in front of her. "We're going to need one of these for the baby."

She stared at it for several seconds, then ran a finger over the small harness. "I don't know what to say."

"It's easy to hook up," he said. "Just takes seconds. An indicator goes from red to green when it's installed correctly." He couldn't tell whether she liked it. "Unlike me, it's idiot proof. But if you want something else, we can return it."

"No," she said quickly. "It's fantastic. The one I wanted. But I don't understand. What does this mean? You keep saying 'we,' but—"

It was time for part two of his screw-up redemption plan. "Erica, I have a million questions about how to be a good father, but zero doubts about you and me."

"But I thought the other night— You made it clear you didn't want this."

He shook his head. "You assumed that and then walked out before we could talk about it."

"You're not wrong." Her hazel eyes were huge as she looked at him, then glanced at the others in the room who were watching this conversation unfold with undisguised curiosity. "But you want to talk about this *now*?"

"Yes. I've waited too long already." He sat in the chair beside hers. "I'm not bailing on you. Not walking away from you. Not now, not ever. I want to be a father to this baby."

"Really?" Her expression was hopeful, but she didn't seem convinced he was all in.

"Yes, really. I've had feelings for you since the first moment I saw you. I was falling for you before I even realized you were pregnant. Love at first sight." He couldn't believe he hadn't put his feelings into words before now. And it was way past time. "I love you, Erica. I love the baby you're carrying. And that makes it my baby, too. I want to be your husband, and I very much want to be his or her father."

"Morgan—" Her voice caught and she swallowed. "I don't know what to say."

"That's because I haven't asked you anything yet." He took the velvet jeweler's box from the front pocket of his jeans. He opened it to reveal the ring he'd picked out at the jewelry store. Angelique, the jewelry designer, had assured him this was the one that would dazzle any woman. He needed the dazzle and a little razzle to convince Erica he was worth taking a chance on.

So, he went down on one knee and said, "Will you make me the happiest man on the planet and marry me? Make a family with me? In case there's any question, the only correct answer is yes."

"Oh, Morgan—"

He waited for her to finish that statement, then couldn't stand it. "Is that an 'Oh, Morgan, I wish you hadn't asked'? Or, 'Oh, Morgan, that's a big fat yes'?"

"It's an 'Oh, Morgan, I love you so much' followed by a heartfelt and unqualified 'absolutely yes.' Nothing would make me happier than to marry you and be a family."

"Thank you, God." He stood and pulled her up and into his arms. The baby kicked just then, and the miracle of it took his breath away. This time there was no doubt or hesitation when he put his hand on her belly. He smiled into her eyes. "I believe our daughter approves."

"Oh? You think we're having a girl?"

"There are five boys in my family. Six with Robby. We're definitely having a girl."

She smiled tenderly. "You are a remarkable man, Morgan Dalton. And I am the luckiest woman in the world. I love you so much."

"I love you more."

And he kissed her, trying to prove just how deeply he meant those words. When they finally came up for air, the expectant dads shook his hand and their wives were sniffling. All of them blamed hormones, but Carla was brushing tears off her cheeks, too, and she wasn't pregnant. The fact of the matter was that everyone loved a happily ever after.

Epilogue

The first Saturday in November, Erica was in her childhood bedroom getting ready for her wedding. She and Morgan wanted to be married before the baby came. Her dream of marriage then baby was coming true after all, though not in the most traditional sense.

Her dress was ivory silk with a lace bodice and long sleeves. The skirt was empire and fell over her tummy and gracefully to the floor. A simple lace veil trailed down her back, secured by a comb in her hair.

Mel, her maid of honor, was fussing with it, making sure the material lay perfectly. She was wearing a lacy, tea-length royal blue dress with a flirty, flared skirt. When she straightened, they stood side by side and looked in the mirror together. And grinned.

"You look beautiful," her almost sister-in-law said.

"Being completely happy does that to a girl."

"This whole bridal thing really suits you."

"When it's right, it's right." She sighed. "With Morgan it was love at first sight. Somehow I knew I would love him forever and beyond."

Mel nodded. "I mean, how can you not be crazy about a guy who proposes with a very impressive diamond ring in one hand and an infant carrier in the other?"

Erica laughed. "He's very special and I'm a lucky girl."

Mel took her hands and squeezed them. "You so deserve the best, and Morgan is that for you."

There was a knock on the door just before her mother opened it. When she saw her daughter, her expression turned achingly tender as her eyes glistened with tears. "Oh, sweetie, you look so beautiful."

"Thank you, Mama."

"And you're not the least bit nervous."

"No room for nerves. Not when I'm so full of happiness. I can't wait to be Mrs. Morgan Dalton."

"Okay, then. Let's get this show on the road. I came up here to let you know the car just arrived to take us to the church." Her mother headed to the door. "Your father and Gabe are already there waiting for us."

"Mama, just real quick before we go—"

"What, sweetie?"

Erica moved close and pulled her into a hug. "I just want to thank you for making today happen. For putting up with me through good and bad. And for being the best mom in the world." She pressed a hand to her belly. "If I'm half as good as you are, I'll do right by this little one."

"You're going to be a wonderful mother. I love you." Angela smiled but her mouth trembled for just a moment. "You're going to make me cry and ruin my makeup."

"I'm sorry, but I needed to say it."

Over the years there'd been ups and downs in their relationship. But the bonds between them were stronger now than ever.

"Okay, ladies," her mom said, "let's get moving."

Erica followed the other two women down the stairs. The house was decorated with flowers for a small reception following the ceremony. Her mother had hired Brittany to handle the event, and Erica already knew that woman could make a feast out of bread and water.

She picked up her bouquet from the box on the entryway table. It was made up of greens and white roses with several orange ones to add a pop of fall color. Mel took her own bouquet, a smaller version of Erica's and they left the house, then stepped into the waiting town car.

A short time later the three of them arrived at the small white church with its graceful, elegant spire. It was charming and traditional and completely perfect. In the vestibule Brittany was waiting for them, looking tall and chic in a pale pink sheath dress with her hair smoothly pulled back into a side bun. Robby was by her side, dapper in his little dark suit and tie, and holding a pillow with two rings. They were symbolic since Morgan's best man had the real ones. And then she saw her father, so handsome in his black suit and tie.

"Hi, Daddy."

"Baby girl—" He stopped and swallowed. "I'm not sure I can give you away."

She moved closer, then stood on tiptoe and kissed his cheek. "You're not. You're just relieved of duty. I have a good man who will be there for me every day, every step of the way."

"I know. Otherwise I wouldn't be able to part with you."

"Okay," Brittany said, taking charge as she gave them all a critical once-over. "Believe it or not, so far everything has gone off without a hitch."

"Of course," Erica said. "You wouldn't accept anything less."

"Darn right." She gave Erica a final approving look. "You ready?"

"Absolutely." She grinned at the boy who would very soon be her nephew. "Robby Dalton, you look awfully handsome."

"Grandma says it runs in the family." The boy gave Brittany a wary look. "My dad and Uncle Morgan told me I have to do everything *she* says."

"They're right." But Brittany smiled at him. "You're going to do great."

Just then the vestibule doors opened, and Gabe walked in. When he saw Erica, a tender look of approval slid into his eyes. But when his gaze settled on his fiancée, he was speechless. Finally he said to her, "Next summer this will be us."

Mel blew him a kiss. "I can't wait."

"Hold that thought, you two. It's time to do *this* wedding," Brittany said. "The groom's mother is already seated. Gabe, escort your mother down the aisle."

He held out his arm and Angela took it. The doors remained open when he walked her down to the front row.

"You ready, Robby?"

The boy looked up at Brittany. "Yes, ma'am."

The organist in the choir loft started playing the traditional "Wedding March," and Robby confidently walked down the aisle, followed by Mel.

"You're up, bride." Brittany hugged her quickly, then brushed away a tear. "You look radiant. Go be happy."

"Thank you. For everything."

Erica took her father's arm, and he put his hand over hers as they matched their steps to the music. She smiled at people as she passed them on her way to the altar. Her groom stood there with his father by his side. Morgan had asked him to be best man, and his mother had cried more than a few happy tears over that.

Then she looked only at Morgan, and he was looking back at her as if she was the most beautiful woman in the world. He sure made her feel that way. In his dark suit and royal blue silk tie, the man defined the word *handsome*, but he was and always would be her cowboy. Eagerly they said their vows and made forever promises that felt so very right.

After pictures, everyone came back to the Ambling A for the reception. Furniture had been moved out of the living and great rooms and tables set up. There were white tablecloths and flowers and a cocktail hour before dinner.

At the family table Malone looked a little uncomfortable being a guest instead of doing the cooking. But Erica had insisted he enjoy her wedding, too. And he'd pronounced the catered food not bad.

There was a dance area on the patio where they shared their first dance as husband and wife. Morgan held out his hand, and she put hers in his palm, knowing somehow that this would never get old.

Afterward he led her back to the family table,

where Gabe and Mel were sitting with her parents and Grandpa Alex. She took the seat beside Malone, who she swore was trying to hide that he was brushing away a tear.

"Sure do wish Josiah could be here to see how pretty his great-granddaughter is."

"I believe he's here in spirit." She leaned her head against his shoulder for a moment.

Then the DJ started talking. "The bride requested a song, a real oldie. It's a tradition at Abernathy weddings. Her great-grandfather, Josiah Abernathy, had it played at his wedding to Cora. Her grandfather did the same as did her parents, George and Angela. So, without further ado, here we go."

The strains of the music began and when the lyrics kicked in, all the guests began to sing along.

"Daisy, Daisy, give me your answer do—" They finished with a rousing, "But you'll look sweet upon the seat of a bicycle built for two."

"Holy cow." Malone sat up straight and sounded very excited. "Holy cow, that's it!"

Erica had never heard that tone from the normally reserved, unflappable man. "What's it?"

"The name I couldn't remember. The name Josiah said when he was talking about the prettiest little girl in the world. It was Daisy."

Erica let that sink in for a moment, then she quivered with excitement. She looked at Gabe and Mel, whose expressions mirrored her own. "Call me crazy, but I don't think he was talking about a girlfriend."

Her brother nodded. "Unless I miss my guess, that's his daughter's name. Her adoptive name."

Erica gripped her new husband's hand. "And I bet Gramps had that song at his wedding as a way to keep his daughter a part of him and his family in any way he could."

"This may be the piece of information we needed," Gabe said. "I'll clue Amanda in right away and we can continue the search." He and Melanie went to find her.

"Way to go, Malone," Erica said.

"Glad I could help. Finally. I need a drink." He got up and went to the bar, and the rest of her family followed.

So, Erica was alone with her new husband and grinned at him. "Do I know how to clear a table, or what?"

"It's your superpower." He smiled, then kissed her.

She was breathless when he stopped. "I aim to please."

"So that song is a family tradition?"

"It is. And I wanted all the Abernathy customs today, because we didn't start out in the most traditional way."

"That song worked in more ways than one." Then he put his hand on her abdomen and smiled at the baby's movement. "And you'd look sweet anywhere, but we need something more family friendly than a bicycle built for two."

"I like the way you think."

It took a very special man to so completely embrace raising a child he didn't make, and her heart was full of emotion. "I love the man you are. You have a heart as big as the Montana sky, Morgan Dalton, and you really stepped up. You'll be an incredible daddy."

"I had no choice," he said. "I made a promise to you. And then I fell in love." He kissed her softly, then met her gaze. "And this cowboy always keeps his promises."

* * * * *

Look for
His Christmas Cinderella
by Christy Jeffries
the next book in the new
Harlequin Special Edition continuity
Montana Mavericks:
What Happened to Beatrix?
On sale November 2020, wherever
Harlequin books and ebooks are sold.

And catch up with the previous
Montana Mavericks titles:

In Search of the Long-Lost Maverick
by New York Times bestselling author
Christine Rimmer

The Cowboy's Comeback
by Melissa Senate

The Maverick's Baby Arrangement
by Kathy Douglass

Available now!

**WE HOPE YOU ENJOYED
THIS BOOK FROM**

**HARLEQUIN
SPECIAL
EDITION**

Believe in love. Overcome obstacles. Find happiness.

Relate to finding comfort and strength in the
support of loved ones and enjoy the journey
no matter what life throws your way.

6 NEW BOOKS AVAILABLE EVERY MONTH!

HSEHALO2020

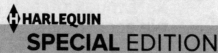
#2797 HIS CHRISTMAS CINDERELLA
Montana Mavericks: What Happened to Beatrix?
by Christy Jeffries

Jordan Taylor has it all—except someone to share his life with. What he really wants for Christmas is to win the heart of Camilla Sanchez, the waitress he met at a charity ball. Camilla thinks they are too different to make it work, but Jordan is determined to prove her wrong—in three weeks!

#2798 SOMETHING ABOUT THE SEASON
Return to the Double C • by Allison Leigh

When wealthy investor Gage Stanton arrives at Rory McAdams's struggling guest ranch, she's suspicious. Is he just there to learn the ranching ropes or to get her to give up the property? But their holiday fling soon begins to feel like anything but—until Gage's shocking secret threatens to derail it.

#2799 THE LONG-AWAITED CHRISTMAS WISH
Dawson Family Ranch • by Melissa Senate

Maisey Clark, a struggling single mom, isn't going to suddenly start believing in Christmas magic. So what if Rex Dawson found her childhood letter to Santa and wants to give her and her daughter the best holiday ever? He's just passing through, and love is for suckers. If only his kisses didn't feel like the miracle she always hoped for...

#2800 MEET ME UNDER THE MISTLETOE
Match Made in Haven • by Brenda Harlen

Haylee Gilmore *always* made practical decisions—except for one unforgettable night with Trevor Blake! Now she's expecting his baby, and the corporate cowboy wants to do the right thing. But the long-distance mom-to-be refuses to marry for duty—she wants his heart.

#2801 A SHERIFF'S STAR
Home to Oak Hollow • by Makenna Lee

Oak Hollow, Texas, was supposed to be a temporary stop between Tess's old life in Boston and the new one in Houston. But when her daughter, Hannah, wraps handsome police chief Anson Curry—who also happens to be their landlord—around her little finger, Tess is tempted for the first time in a long time.

#2802 THEIR CHRISTMAS BABY CONTRACT
Blackberry Bay • by Shannon Stacey

With IVF completely out of her financial reach, Reyna Bishop is running out of time to have the child she so very much wants. Her deal with Brady Nash is purely practical: no emotion, no expectation, no ever-after. It's foolproof...till the time she spends with Brady and his warm, loving family leaves Reyna wanting more than a baby...

Oak Hollow, Texas, was supposed to be a temporary stop between Tess's old life in Boston and the new one in Houston, which includes her daughter's lifesaving heart surgery. But when Hannah wraps handsome police chief Anson Curry—who also happens to be their landlord—around her little finger, Tess is tempted for the first time in a long time.

Read on for a sneak peek at
A Sheriff's Star
by debut author Makenna Lee,
the first book in her Home to Oak Hollow series!

"Sweet dreams, little one," he said and stepped out of the room.

She took off Hannah's shoes and jeans, then tucked her in for the night. With a bolstering breath, she braced herself for being alone with her fantasy man.

He stood in the center of the living room, looking around like he'd never seen his own house. She followed Anson's gaze to the built-in shelves she'd filled with precious and painful memories. Things she wasn't ready to share with him. Before he could ask any questions, she opened the front door.